"Let's Get One Thing Straight. Married Or Not, I Don't Intend To Get Naked And Play Bride And Groom With You."

Josh smiled. "Fair enough. And I'll try not to play ravishing pirate to your outraged captive."

A tide of pink rose from Cari's shoulders to her neck to her cheeks. But she still answered him bluntly. "Try hard, Mr. Keegan. Try *very* hard."

"We're on our honeymoon, remember? Don't you think you should call me Josh?"

"I can think of several things I'd like to call you." She shot him a straight look. "Please don't make this situation worse by turning on the charm. I don't know how to handle it...or you."

"I'd say you handle both pretty well," he replied.

Dear Reader,

This month, we begin HOLIDAY HONEYMOONS, a wonderful new cross-line continuity series written by two of your favorites—Merline Lovelace and Carole Buck. The series begins in October with Merline's *Halloween Honeymoon*. Then, once a month right through February, look for holiday love stories by Merline and Carole—in Desire for November, Intimate Moments for December, back to Desire in January and concluding in Intimate Moments for Valentine's Day. Sound confusing? It's not—we'll keep you posted as the series continues…and I personally guarantee that these books are keepers!

And there are other goodies in store for you. Don't miss the fun as Cathie Linz's delightful series THREE WEDDINGS AND A GIFT continues with *Seducing Hunter*. And Lass Small's MAN OF THE MONTH, *The Texas Blue Norther*, is simply scrumptious.

Those of you who want an *ultrasensuous* love story need look no further than *The Sex Test* by Patty Salier. She's part of our WOMEN TO WATCH program highlighting brand-new writers. Warning: this book is HOT!

Readers who can't get enough of cowboys shouldn't miss Anne Marie Winston's *Rancher's Baby*. And if you're partial to a classic amnesia story (as I certainly am!), be sure to read Barbara McCauley's delectable *Midnight Bride*.

And, as always, I'm here to listen to you—so don't be afraid to write and tell me your thoughts about Desire!

Until next month,

Lucia Macro

Senior Editor

Please address questions and book requests to:
Silhouette Reader Service
U.S.: 3010 Walden Ave., P.O. Box 1325, Buffalo, NY 14269
Canadian: P.O. Box 609, Fort Erie, Ont. L2A 5X3

MERLINE LOVELACE
HALLOWEEN HONEYMOON

SILHOUETTE *Desire*
Published by Silhouette Books
America's Publisher of Contemporary Romance

SILHOUETTE BOOKS

ISBN 0-373-76030-2

HALLOWEEN HONEYMOON

MERLINE LOVELACE,

after serving twenty-three exciting, adventure-filled years as an officer in the United States Air Force, retired and began a second, equally exciting career as a romance novelist. She and her husband, who also retired from the Air Force and has since begun his own second career as an antique dealer, love travel, antiquing and golf—not necessarily in that order!

Halloween Honeymoon is the first in the fun-filled, five-book HOLIDAY HONEYMOONS series. Watch for the next book in the series, *Thanksgiving Honeymoon*, coming next month from Silhouette Desire.

Merline enjoys hearing from readers and can be reached at P.O. Box 892717, Oklahoma City, OK 73189.

To Merl, who convinced Al and me to take up the sport
of kings almost ten years ago. Thanks, Dad, for all those
wonderful hours in the sun and the fresh air, chasing
silly white balls in and out of sand traps.

Prologue

"**H**ey, Lucy, wait till you take a look-see at the prize package I put together for the Halloween Charity Ball tonight."

Lucy Falco, office manager of Gulliver's Travels, glanced up from her blinking computer screen at the agency's newest employee. A short-order cook turned used-car salesman turned travel agent, Jim Burns had proved to be enthusiastic, and surprisingly adept at his new career.

"What do you have?" she asked, smiling.

"It's a honey of a deal." Eagerly he passed her a glossy brochure. "I convinced the owner of the *Nautilus III* to give us the VIP suite for a ten-day cruise."

Lucy's dark brows lifted as she stared at a color photo of a sleek, incredibly sybaritic white yacht anchored in a turquoise bay fringed with feathery green palms.

"I don't know, Jim," she said doubtfully. "Even at a substantial discount, this package has got to be more than the target the boss set for our donation."

"No, it's not. It's less than half."

"You're kidding!"

"The owner's hoping to expand and needs referrals. Look, here's the fax from him confirming the offer."

Drawn by his excitement, several of the other agents crowded around while Lucy studied the confirmation from the owner and skipper of the *Nautilus III*. As Jim had stated, the figures for the cruise package were amazingly low.

Too low.

"There's got to be a catch," Lucy murmured, frowning as she studied the figures with serious brown eyes.

"No, it's all here in black and white. The package includes airfare to Miami, luxury accommodations and all meals."

Another agent, with a wild mane of silvery-white curls, a smooth complexion that belied her sixty-plus years and the impossible name of Tiffany Tarrington Toulouse, beamed at her fellow employee.

"What a coup, Jim! Mr. Gulliver will be so pleased. He was one of the original organizers of this charity ball in support of the Special Olympics. He always wants our contribution to be extraspecial."

Her mascaraed eyes rounded as she studied the brochure Lucy passed her. "Good heavens, this yacht is twice the size of my house. And look at the Jacuzzi on the sun deck. Whoever takes this prize package home tonight is going to be one lucky person!''

One

Cari O'Donnell placed her skull-shaped mug of gruesome green punch on a tray stand and edged behind a pillar. Turning her back on the noisy, costumed crowd filling the ballroom of Atlanta's Doubletree Hotel, she grasped the edge of her bodice and tugged it up.

Or tried to.

The darned thing wouldn't budge.

Cari let out as much of a sigh as the constrictive bodice would allow. Here she'd been so thrilled to actually wear the lavish costume she'd constructed in such exact detail as part of her doctoral research! The black velvet gown featured a low, square-cut neckline, puffed, slashed sleeves, and a full skirt draped over an oblong hoop. To add to the gold lace trim edging the front, she'd draped a long rope of *faux* pearls around her neck and and loaded her fingers with rings. As a final touch, she'd moussed her fly-away bangs straight back from her forehead and pinned up her shoulder-length honey-colored hair in a style right out of the sixteenth century. In her professional opinion, she looked gloriously Elizabethan.

Unfortunately, she hadn't been able to take a full breath since she'd hooked herself into the darn dress. The board-stiff bodice flattened the bottom halves of her breasts into thin pancakes and plumped the top halves to high, quivering mounds. She'd spent her entire time at the party maneuvering her wide skirts through the crowd and worrying that she'd pop right out of the lung-compressing bodice. What was more, she wasn't used to the kind of sidelong masculine glances her dramatic cleavage had been snaring.

The next time she attended a costume ball, Cari thought wryly, she'd opt for comfort instead of historical accuracy. She gave the bodice another futile yank.

"Need some help?"

The deep, roguish drawl just behind her left shoulder brought Cari spinning around—*not* a wise move for a woman wearing four-inch-high platform shoes modeled after their sixteenth-century counterparts. Tilting crazily, she lost her balance and tumbled into two quickly outstretched arms.

They folded around her, bringing her up against a broad expanse of bare chest. Cari clutched at firm, well-muscled arms, covered in soft white cotton, afraid to move. She had no idea what might have become dislodged in her sudden movement, and wasn't quite ready to find out. She leaned against the solid chest wall for a few moments, wrinkling her nose as a tuft of dark, springy hair tickled it.

The well-muscled torso under her cheek told Cari instantly whose arms she'd fallen into. She'd noticed only one bare-chested pirate among the throngs of Draculas and masked Zorros and Headless Horsemen at the Halloween Charity Ball. She'd also noticed the six feet or more of throat-closing, heart-stopping masculinity that went with the eye patch and billowing white shirt open to the waist.

Cari might have sworn off any involvement with the male of the species for the foreseeable future, but she wasn't nerve-dead from the neck down—contrary to her ex-fiancé's snide remark during their last, stormy encounter! She was woman enough to recognize a superb biological specimen when she saw one.

Or felt one.

Her heart thumping, she tilted her head back and stared up into a tanned, outrageously handsome face topped by wavy dark hair. One hazel eye gleamed down at her wickedly. The other—also hazel, she had to assume—was covered by the black patch.

Oh, God, he was as incredible close up as he'd appeared when she first spotted him across the crowded ballroom. A modern-day pirate to his teeth, despite his hopelessly inaccurate costume. If she'd been capable of speech at that moment, Cari could have told him that tight black pants and this revealing white shirt constituted a Hollywood image of the brethren that had little basis in historical fact. But this man didn't require a costume to qualify for the brotherhood of rogues. His slashing grin and that wicked glint in his eye were all the credentials he needed.

Cari knew who he was, of course. She'd recognized him the moment he strolled into the ballroom. So had every other woman at the ball. Josh Keegan. Atlanta's homegrown and most popular celebrity. Pro golfer and dedicated bachelor, who thoroughly enjoyed his freewheeling life-style, if the many stories printed about him in the tabloids were to be believed.

A historian by inclination and profession, Cari knew little about sports and nothing at all about golf. Her only contact with athletes were the jocks in the freshman Western Civ course she taught. Had taught, she corrected, remembering her currently unemployed status with a slight grimace.

Yet even historians had to stand in line at the grocery store. Over the past few years, the supermarket gossip sheets had regularly splashed Josh Keegan's handsome face and athletic form across their front pages—usually with a different female draped over his arm or staring up adoringly at him.

The same tabloids had gone wild over Keegan's injury a few months ago. Huge headlines had speculated about whether the ball that sliced out of the woods, shattered his sunglasses and drove shards of plastic into his left eye had been hit by another golfer, a jealous husband or a malevolent supernatural force. Whatever or whoever had propelled the missile, the resulting injury had left Josh Keegan with an eye patch that only added to his rakish air and bad-boy charm.

A charm he now turned up to its full megawatt power. His mouth, only inches from Cari's own, tilted lazily. White teeth gleamed against skin tanned to a polished oak.

"Sorry. I didn't mean to startle you. Are you okay?"

Swallowing, she eased away from his chest the merest fraction and glanced down. She was still in her gown. More or less.

"Yes," she replied in relief. "I'm fine."

She pulled back a little more, only to halt abruptly as the gold lace at the lower edge of her V-shaped bodice snagged on his elaborate belt buckle. Instinctively she canted her hips into his to keep from tearing the rare antique trim.

At her movement, his grin deepened. The potent impact of that all male smile collapsed Cari's lungs. Or maybe it was the way his hands roamed her velvet-covered spine that drove the air completely out of her. Or her too-tight bodice. At this point, all she knew was that her respiratory system had completely shut down.

"I, uh, think we're caught," she got out somehow.

"I think you are."

There was no mistaking the suggestive glint in his eye. Flustered, Cari leaned away from him.

"Careful," he cautioned. "You'll tear it."

Shifting slightly, he settled her more firmly between his muscular thighs—no mean trick, considering the fact that the oblong cage supporting her skirt was almost a yard wide. With the movement, her hoop dipped down in front and rose up in back. Cool air washed against Cari's calves above her twentieth-century knee-highs. The thought of someone noticing her costuming anachronism flustered her as much as being pressed so intimately against Josh Keegan's groin.

Ha! Who was she kidding?

"I hate to be the one to break it to you, Scarlett," he drawled, amusement lacing his deep voice as he took in the hump of material rising behind her, "but your hoop's all bent out of shape. It's a lot wider than it is round."

"It's supposed to be. It's a farthingale."

"You could have fooled me."

The teasing note in his voice sent tiny ripples of pleasure across Cari's bare skin. She wet her lips, totally disconcerted by his effect on her.

"It's not a hoopskirt such as women wore in the antebellum South," she explained. "This style originated at the court of Castile in the late 1400s."

His amusement deepened as his gaze swept her exaggerated width. "Leave it to the folks who invented the Inquisition to come up with something like this to protect their ladies' virtue."

"Actually," Cari replied, squirming a bit, "Queen Juana designed it to disguise a pregnancy from her incapacitated husband, Enrique V."

He eyed the hooped material with new respect. "No kidding?"

She should have expected Josh Keegan to appreciate that bit of historical trivia. By all accounts, Queen Juana's reputation for playing the field paled beside his.

"No kidding," she replied.

Cari couldn't quite believe she was tethered to a man most women would pay dearly to be tied to, carrying on a conversation about hooped skirts. Gingerly she leaned as far back in his arms as she could without tearing the fragile lace.

"If you'll hold still a moment, I'll disengage."

"I'll do my best, sweetheart."

Ignoring both his easy familiarity and the way his gaze lingered on her décolletage, she slid her hands between their bodies. At the brush of her knuckles against his warm skin, his stomach hollowed.

Cari's lurched.

This was ridiculous, she told herself sternly, fumbling with the lace snagged on his belt buckle. Not three months ago, she'd plopped her engagement ring and her resignation on her fiancé's desk, then walked out of his office. She'd been subsisting on her savings since then, burying herself in her research while she waited to hear about the grant she'd applied for from the Atlanta History Center.

She hadn't come up for air in weeks. She certainly wouldn't have attended this elegant charity ball, where the price of admission was more than she earned in a week—used to earn!—if she hadn't served as a volunteer coordinator for the Special Olympics this summer and received a free ticket in the mail. The chance to dress up for a few hours in the gown she'd copied in such excruciating detail had been too delicious to resist.

Dressing up was one thing, however. Standing here while a modern-day pirate undressed her with his eyes was something else again.

She had no business going all weak-kneed and breathless over a male, even if this one was as different from her former fiancé as sinfully rich chocolate was from fat-free, cholesterol-free rice cakes. Trying not to touch any more of the warm, leathery skin of his stomach than she had to, Cari worried the lace to free it from the ornate buckle.

"Suck it in," she ordered, nibbling on her lower lip in concentration.

The golden skin under her hands rippled with laughter. "It's in as far as it will go. I'm a little out of shape these days."

If he was out of shape, Cari thought, every other man in the room was in serious trouble.

"I've almost got it, Mr. Keegan. Just hold still a moment."

"You know who I am?"

His breath washed against her cheek, warm and husky with the scent of the rum or whiskey or whatever had been used to spike the bubbling green punch.

"Doesn't everyone?" Cari returned, concentrating on her task. "Your picture's on every ad and poster advertising this charity ball. You are the celebrity host of this event, after all."

"Right, that's me. The celebrity host."

The strange catch in his words made her glance up. Before she could decide what might have caused it, another voice carried over the noise of the crowd.

"Hey, Josh, I've been looking all over the place for you."

"Go away, Oglethorpe."

"But we need our big celebrity to start the auction for the— Oh! Ex*cuse* me."

Cari peered around Keegan's shoulder to see a tall, silver-haired man in striped prison garb, complete with ball and chain dangling from one hand. The newcomer's mouth curved as he took in their intimate embrace.

"Fast work, Josh, even for you."

"Get lost, Billy Bob," Keegan instructed, not bothering to turn around.

Billy Bob? Gulping, Cari recognized the state's lieutenant governor, William Robert Oglethorpe.

"Well, I'd like to, ol' buddy," he replied, chuckling. "But we came here tonight to raise some cold hard cash, remember? Think you can let your prize go long enough to get with it?"

"No can do," Keegan replied, grinning down at Cari. "We're hooked."

"Josh Keegan, hooked?" Oglethorpe hooted in derision. "That's something I'd like to see."

"Me too!" another voice boomed.

What was this? Cari thought in embarrassment. A meeting of the Josh Keegan fan club? Twisting her head, she saw a red-suited devil with a three-pronged pitchfork join their little group. His tufted black brows soared upward when he noticed her hands playing with Keegan's belt. Heat warmed her cheeks as she realized she was adding another notch to Josh Keegan's reputation.

"Seeing Josh bite the dust is something a good number of us would pay to see," the lieutenant governor said, chuckling. "I don't know what it is about a confirmed bachelor that makes every married man ache to see him shackled."

He rattled his ball and chain to emphasize his point. Lucifer stared at him for a moment, then thumped the floor with the end of his pitchfork in sudden enthusiasm.

"Hey, you've got something there, Billy Bob! Instead of auctioning off a bunch of prizes no one needs or particularly wants tonight, let's auction off Josh."

He gave Cari a sideways glance. "Or better yet, marry him off, since he appears to have already found a partner."

"Wait a minute, Harry," Keegan protested. "Let's not get carried away here."

"Trust me, Josh, it's a great idea," the devil insisted. "We'll stage a mock ceremony and collect 'wedding presents' from the guests, all of which will be donated to the Special Olympics. I'm telling you, we'll raise a bundle."

"Sounds good to me," the felonious legislator put in. "Come on, Josh. You've done a lot crazier stunts in your time."

"Well..."

"It might sound good to you gentlemen," Cari put in, a little piqued at the way the three men assumed she'd fall in with their scheme. "You can marry Mr. Keegan off if you wish, but you'll have to find him another bride. I'm not in the market for a groom right now."

Not now, and not anytime in the near future. Maybe after the next presidential election. Or the next appearance of Halley's comet. Whichever came later.

"But you're so well matched," Lucifer protested. "The lady and the pirate. The Spanish noblewoman and the buccaneer who carries her off."

Cari didn't bother to point out that the elaborate embroidery on her costume made it distinctly English in style, not Spanish. Or that she had no intention of being carried off by anyone. She fumbled with the lace caught on Keegan's belt buckle, wanting out of this ridiculous situation.

"Come on," Satan coaxed, in much the same voice he might have used with Eve. "It's just a gag."

Ignoring him, Cari gave the lace a tug, then winced when it tore free. She'd paid far more for the trim than she could afford, but once she spotted it in a musty antique store in Savannah, she'd had to have it. Still, she wasn't about to let it bind her, even symbolically, to any man.

Freed of her tether, she tried to step back. To her surprise, Keegan's hold didn't slacken. She glanced up to find his eyes—correction, his eye—on her chest. Correction, her cleavage.

Another wave of heat washed up Cari's neck at the gleam of masculine appreciation in its hazel depths. Hard on the heels of her embarrassment came a lowering thought.

Maybe Edward had been right. Maybe she'd devoted herself and her studies to the wrong century. The wrong culture. The Elizabethans had been bold, bawdy and blunt. Cari, in her former fiancé's considered opinion, qualified for only one out of three. Impulsiveness didn't equate with boldness in Edward's book. And she had too many inhibitions to shed before she came anywhere close to bawdy. She would've been more at home a century or two later, he'd told her. Among the Puritans.

Blunt, however, she could manage.

"I don't want to marry you, Mr. Keegan. Any more than you want to marry me."

"I don't know," he murmured, his hands roving her back. "The idea's kind of growing on me."

The glinting laughter in his gold-flecked eye told Cari he was playing with her. She should have been annoyed. She should have pulled out of his hold. She should have told all three men to get real. She had every intention of doing just that when Keegan dropped his arms and stood back.

"What do you say, Miss—?" He lifted a brow. "Or is it Mrs.?"

"It's Ms.," she replied, refusing to admit that she instantly missed the feel of his arms around her. Was she an idiot, or what? "O'Donnell. Caren O'Donnell. Cari to my friends."

Lucifer and the felon exchanged glances, smirking over the fact that two people who'd been wrapped around each other like kudzu vines until a few seconds ago hadn't bothered with introductions.

"Well, I'd say a prospective groom might qualify as a friend. What do you say, Cari? It's for a good cause. Shall we do it?"

In the face of his good-natured willingness to go along with the scheme, she found it difficult to refuse without sounding churlish. It *was* for a good cause, one she believed in.

"Well," she replied slowly, "I think the whole idea's silly, but I suppose I can play along."

The devil banged his pitchfork against the floor in delight. "Great! Billy Bob, you can give the bride away. Come on, Josh, let's go announce your imminent nuptials. Then I'll have to find a cardinal or a bishop or someone to perform the ceremony."

He dragged Keegan away before Cari had time for second thoughts. Which she did. Immediately. Second, and third, and fourth thoughts. But her pride wouldn't let her admit that the idea of a fake wedding ceremony stung just a bit. More than a bit.

Okay, so she'd learned the hard way that Edward wasn't the man for her? So she'd begun to suspect it even before she discovered that he'd used her research in the paper he presented to the American Historical Society? So a niggling sense of relief at her close escape had begun to edge out her anger in recent weeks? Still, she'd spent one whole summer planning a future with him.

Their wedding would have been a small, elegant affair, Cari mused as waves of delighted laughter greeted the devil's announcement of Josh Keegan's imminent transition from carefree bachelor to careworn spouse. Tuning out Satan's cheerfully blunt demands for generous "wedding gifts," Cari swallowed and thought about what might have been.

They'd intended to invite only the family and a few close friends. Her parents would have flown in from Indiana, and her dad would have given her away. Cari would have worn an antique lace mantilla with a tealength dress in soft, creamy satin. Afterward, she would have held a small reception. She'd planned to serve champagne and the heavenly spice cake baked by her neighbor, Mrs. Wilder.

She would *not* have walked down an aisle formed by a grinning crowd of bumblebees and clowns and Frankensteins. She would *not* have clutched the arm of a felon. She most certainly would *not* have found a half-naked pirate waiting for her at the end of the aisle.

Flicking the pirate in question a quick look, Cari was struck by the differences between her pretend groom and her almost-groom. Dry-witted and at times acerbic, Edward had cultivated a properly professorial, distinguished air. Josh Keegan, on the other hand, possessed an overabundance of charm and carried himself with the natural grace of a professional athlete.

Tall, tanned and too darn handsome for his own good, he towered over Lucifer on the low stage. Light from the chandeliers burnished his dark hair to the luster of polished teak. His billowy white shirt gave tantalizing glimpses of shoulders and arms that were smooth and well muscled, as Cari could personally attest. Tight black pants shaped narrow hips and strong thighs.

Strangely, though, his easy, laughing manner stirred her far more than his admittedly awesome physical attributes. He joked with the crowd and with the devil, whose skill at extracting money made Cari suspect he was either the event's organizer or a very good lawyer, or both. As she watched from the sidelines, pledges began to pour in. After some spirited give-and-take, a smiling dark-haired woman with the pointed ears, quivering whiskers and sleek body of a black cat stepped to the microphone.

"In recognition of this momentous occasion, Gulliver's Travels has converted the grand prize for best costume into a honeymoon cruise."

Laughter swelled through the crowd, and someone yelled that they should christen the ship the *Titanic II*, since Josh Keegan was about to go under.

"This package is for the participants, for being such good sports," the woman announced with a lively smile. "Mr. Gulliver has authorized me to match the cost of the cruise with a donation to the Special Olympics."

"Way to go!" Lucifer exclaimed.

Thunderous applause greeted her announcement, and more donations followed. When the barrage of wedding presents finally halted, a gleeful Satan announced that the pledges came to almost ten thousand dollars.

Cari gasped. "Ten thousand dollars!"

The idea of raising that much money for a worthwhile cause wiped away her last hesitation. Tossing the memories of her quiet, elegant wedding into a mental trash bin, she managed a smile as the lieutenant governor offered his arm.

"Are you ready?"

"Ready as I'll ever be," she answered, slipping her arm through his.

He signaled to the orchestra, which began a slow, mournful march. It sounded like a dirge, Cari thought. It *was* a dirge, she realized with a start. A full-fledged funeral march. Shaking her head, she clutched the prisoner's arm and started down the aisle.

A fanged Dracula suddenly stepped out of the crowd. "Wait a minute! The bride needs a bouquet."

He plucked a long-stemmed calla lily from the spray decorating the cardboard coffin strapped to his friend's back. Bowing, he handed it to Cari. She murmured her thanks, tucked the waxy flower into the crook of her arm and fell into step once more. With each measured pace that brought her closer to the broad-shouldered buccaneer, her heart thumped painfully against her ribs.

This was only pretend, she reminded herself. Just a gag.

Josh stood on the low platform and watched his bride approach. At the sight of her strained smile and her soft breasts pushing against her costume, he grinned wryly to himself.

Marriage had been the last thing on his mind when he first spotted this pint-size but superbly packaged female. At the time, all he was interested in had been whether she was going to fall out of the gown she kept trying to pull up. When she ducked behind the pillar to give it another yank, he'd followed her on pure instinct. An instinct that had led to this sappy charade.

It might be sappy, Josh reminded himself, but it had raised almost ten grand. And raising money had been his main function tonight as celebrity host.

Celebrity host. The title echoed hollowly in his mind, drowning out the solemn notes of the wedding march.

Christ! Six months ago he'd come in second at the Masters. Four months ago he'd won the British Open, playing the finest round of golf of his life. A week later, a ball had ricocheted out of the woods, and now all he played was charity events like this.

Although he concealed his injury behind an eye patch and his uncertainty about his future behind the lazy grin the media and the groupies loved, Josh was starting to resent the new role he'd been thrust into. He supported a number of causes. Had always done so. But he wasn't quite ready for a full-time career as a celebrity spokesperson for the physically challenged.

He was a golfer. That was all he'd ever been. All he ever wanted to be. The game came as naturally as breathing to him, and he was good at it. Damn good. He refused to believe he wouldn't shake this blurred vision and these blasted headaches and get back on tour.

He'd go through with this final charade for Billy Bob, Josh decided. He owed his boyhood friend that much, and more, for all his support since the accident. But he wouldn't get involved with any more charity events for a while. He needed to start swinging a club again. He needed to reestablish a training regimen, or he'd never make it back to the winner's circle. Shoving the doubts about his future that had plagued him for weeks to the back of his mind, Josh summoned up a grin and forced himself to focus on his bride.

Lord, she was an intriguing bundle of femininity. She glided toward him like a queen, her heavy skirts swishing and her breasts quivering above that ironing board of a dress. Everything about her hinted at rigidly constrained sensuality, from her gown to her wide pansy-brown eyes. The idea of being the one to release her from her constraints, physical and otherwise, added spice to the proceedings.

Maybe, Josh thought with a resurgence of his natural optimism, just maybe, his luck was changing. Maybe he'd find himself enjoying a wedding night, as well as a wedding.

His bride stopped a few feet away, gripping Billy Bob's arm as though it were a lifeline. The bleary-eyed little judge standing beside Josh harrumphed and waited for the funeral march to come to a mournful end.

Josh glanced down at the man garbed as a barrister, wondering where in the world Harry had come up with him. He wore a shiny black robe and a moth-eaten old-fashioned wig that draped over his bald head at an odd angle. He looked, Josh decided, like a refugee from a law-office rummage sale. And if the bourbon fumes wafting from him at regular intervals were any indication, he'd consumed more than his fair share of the potent punch.

When the music ended, the judge squinted at the couple standing before the platform.

"Who—?"

He broke off, swaying to one side. Josh steadied him with a firm hold on his arm. Over the judge's head, he caught his bride's startled look. Then rueful laughter sprang into her brown eyes, and Josh sucked in a quick breath.

Flushed and flustered, Cari O'Donnell had intrigued him. Sparkling with suppressed laughter, she barreled into him like a runaway golf cart.

"Ahem." The judge swiped his tongue across his lips and tried again. "Who gives this woman to be married?"

"I do," Billy Bob announced in ringing tones. He patted the bride's hand, then offered it to Josh.

Cari shivered as strong, callused fingers intertwined with hers and pulled her gently toward the dais. This wasn't real, she reminded herself. Her groom wasn't real. An hour from now, two at the most, she'd be tucked in bed, with her books scattered around her. This would all be a crazy memory to shake her head over. Yet his touch seemed to sear her skin, and she shivered as she stepped up to stand beside him.

"I don't remember all the words," the judge muttered, frowning at the couple before him as though his memory lapse was their fault. "Just the pertinent ones. Do you—?" He squinted up at the groom. "What did you say your name was?"

"Josh. Keegan."

"John?"

"Josh. Joshua."

"Do you, Joshua Keegan, take this woman to have and to hold, and so on and so forth?"

A silence fell, then stretched on. And on!

The crowd tittered. Male voices called last-minute warnings. Female laughter tinkled through the ballroom. The judge crooked his neck, blinking owlishly.

Cari wondered if the world's most determined bachelor would chicken out at this crucial moment. She tilted her head, glancing up at him out of the corner of her eye. He was playing to the crowd, she realized. Or waiting till he'd snagged her full attention. Once he had it, he flashed her another of those lopsided grins that did strange things to her heartbeat.

"I do."

The judge glowered at Cari. "Do you—?"

"Wait a minute!" A surgeon in gore-stained garments stepped forward.

"We're not to that part yet," the barrister snapped. "I'll tell you when you can speak or forever hold your peace."

"But they need a license. And a blood test. I've got a scalpel. Anyone got a pen?"

"No way," Cari protested. She wasn't going to let some nut puncture her, not even for ten thousand dollars in pledges. Not in this day and age. "No scalpels."

"Now see here," the judge said testily, obviously annoyed at being interrupted. "They don't need any license, or a blood test. I'm a retired state supreme court justice. Under the Judiciary Reorganization Act of 1877, I retain full plenipotentiary powers over certain state laws."

The surgeon backed off, laughing. "If you say so, Judge."

Josh was impressed. Despite his tipsy state, the little barrister could think fast enough on his feet. That small matter settled, the judge swung back to Cari.

"Well? Do you?"

"Oh! I . . . I guess so."

"You guess so?" The moth-eaten wig flapped as he shook his head. "Do you or don't you?"

Cari swallowed. "I do."

"By the authority vested in me, and so forth and so forth, I pronounce you man and wife."

That was it? No rings? No stirring words about the sanctity of marriage? The abrupt conclusion left Cari feeling hollow and wondering what they were supposed to do next. She didn't wonder for long.

The judge turned to Josh with a snort. "Well, go ahead and kiss her."

Josh didn't need further prompting. Folding Cari into his arms, he bent her backward with the force of his kiss.

Half laughing, wholly embarrassed, she clung to him, as much to protect her modesty as to keep her balance. Applause thundered around them, giving way to hoots and catcalls as the kiss went on.

And on.

And *on!*

When Josh finally straightened, she was breathless and dizzy and tingling from her head to her toes. What little air she managed to pull into her lungs whooshed out again as he swept her into his arms and carried her out of the ballroom.

TWO

As he traversed the ballroom, Josh discovered that maneuvering a woman wearing a skirt the size of a beach umbrella through a crowd of well-wishers and backslappers was no mean feat. He also discovered that his bride wasn't quite the lightweight she appeared. She linked her arms around his neck for balance, but a nicely rounded bottom bumped against his middle with each step, and her compact body was proving to be an armful. By the time he cleared the ballroom, his breath was rasping in his throat...and not just from the feel of her warm breath on his neck.

Damn! He really was out of shape. The realization threw him, then sharpened to hard resolve his decision of a few moments ago to start swinging a club again. It was time he put his life back in order, he thought grimly. Hefting his bride a little higher, he ignored the small lance of pain just over his left eye that the action caused and strode across the lobby.

"Where are we going, if you don't mind me asking?"

Josh glanced down at the woman in his arms, seeing her in the bright lights of the lobby for the first time. An unexpected pleasure jolted through him. Lord, what skin! All creamy and soft-looking and flushed with pink. Briefly he wondered whether her heightened color was the result of being carried through a busy hotel lobby to the accompaniment of surprised stares and titters of amusement ... or the aftermath of their kiss.

Josh still wasn't quite sure what had happened with that kiss. He'd intended it as a joke, one of the grandstand plays for the crowd that he was famous for, but the joke had boomeranged. Big-time! At the touch of her full mouth on his, sudden, scorching heat had raced through his veins. Even now, the memory of her lips moving under his knotted him so tight it took a real effort to reply to her question.

"I thought we'd better blow the wedding party before Harry started selling ringside seats to our divorce. How about a glass of champagne to toast our newly wedded state?"

"Well ..." She glanced doubtfully at the entrance to the cocktail lounge.

"I'm staying here at the hotel. We can go up to my room and order from room service." A belated thought occurred to him. "Or did you come with someone? Someone who might object to your sudden disappearance?"

"Isn't it a bit late to worry about that?" she replied, lifting one brow.

"Better late than never," Josh countered easily, but his step slowed as he remembered how she'd evaded answering his question earlier about her marital status.

An instinctive caution kicked in, and he halted in front of the elevator. For all his playboy reputation, Josh played this particular game by his own, very private set of rules. Although he'd enjoyed one or two steady relationships in the past few years, his fierce concentration on his sport precluded the kind of wild affairs the media loved to spin into near misses at the altar. Well, it precluded *most* of them. In any case, he'd learned early in his rookie days to avoid destructive triangles with married women.

"Well? Is there someone who might object to our sharing a glass of champagne?"

"No, there isn't."

He had to strain to hear her reply over the buzz of conversation in the lobby. Then her chin tilted upward, and she added, "And yes, I'd like a glass of champagne."

Josh caught the faint hint of defiance in her voice. And the echo of recklessness. He'd heard both before. Too many times not to recognize them instantly. Cari O'Donnell might or might not be married, but she wouldn't object to some fun with a stranger...like most of the groupies who followed the tour.

The sharp sense of disappointment that swept through him took Josh aback. What the heck was the matter with him? So what if she wanted to play games with him for some private purpose of her own? Not ten minutes ago he'd been hoping he'd get lucky and share a mock wedding night, as well as a wedding, with this delectable creature.

That had been before he caught the sparkle of laughter in her wide brown eyes, a perverse corner of his mind argued. Before he kissed her. She'd tasted so fresh, so surprised. So unlike the women who made themselves available at every tournament.

Telling himself he was an idiot for regretting his impulsive offer, Josh hefted her again and stabbed the elevator button with one finger. Her body rolled into his, and Josh felt the swell of her upper breasts against his chest. The feel of those plump, mashed mounds went a long way to easing both his momentary doubts and the familiar pain now pulsing just above his eye.

She righted herself, flushed and laughing. "I appreciate that you swashbuckling types have a reputation to maintain, but I can walk, you know."

The elevator doors whirred open, and a wide-eyed couple stepped out. Josh gave them a quick grin, then carried his prize into the paneled cubicle. As the elevator hummed upward, he leaned his shoulders against the smooth-grained wood and rested her weight on his stomach.

"No sweat," he replied. "If I put you down now, I'd just have to pick you up to carry you over the threshold, and I'm not sure I could manage it again with that satellite dish you're wearing. Besides—" he glanced up at the indicator panel "—we're here."

Cari curled her arm around his neck as he twisted sideways to maneuver her farthingale out of the elevator. Once more she felt the heat and the strength of his body as he strode down a long hallway carpeted in plush mauve and lit by elegant crystal chandeliers. She had to resist the urge to pinch herself. She couldn't quite believe that she was in Josh Keegan's arms. Or that he was carrying her to his hotel room.

She just didn't do things like this.

Not with men like Josh, anyway.

Okay, she could be a bit impulsive at times. Like when she'd sailed out of Edward's office, ignoring little things like car payments and rent and food in her anger and indignation. Or when she'd moved to Georgia in the first place, drawn by the irresistible lure of working with a man considered a leader in her chosen field.

Some leader! Edward had used her and her research shamelessly—kind of like she was using Josh, her conscience snuck in.

Hey, all she wanted was a little conversation with an attractive man. A glass of champagne. A taste of excitement. And maybe another of those soul-shattering kisses, Cari tacked on, her heart thumping.

She wasn't about to indulge in anything more. Not after her recent escape. And certainly not with someone like Josh Keegan, who collected women the way other people collected matchbooks.

The truth! her pesky conscience demanded. Admit it! What she really wanted was the thrill of being swept off her feet for a few moments by a world-class hunk, to counter the sting of Edward's snide comments.

Maybe so. But that wasn't using him. Much. No more than he used the dozens—hundreds!—of women he'd been linked with.

At the thought of being linked, even temporarily, to the man who held her, Cari's blood raced shamelessly. The fingers she'd locked behind his strong, corded neck itched with the urge to thread themselves through his dark hair. The hallway lights brought out the deep red tints hidden amid its casual layers.

"Can you reach my pocket?"

"What?" She dragged her gaze from his hair, to find his hazel eye regarding her with a rueful glint.

"We've made it this far. I hate to spoil my act now by setting you down while I fish for the key. It's in my left pocket. Can you reach it?"

"Uh . . . sure."

Cari loosened her hold and slid her hand down his shoulder to his hip. He shifted slightly so that she could insert her hand in his pants pocket. With *very* careful precision, she fished among the scattered objects she encountered for the flat piece of plastic that would open the safety lock. Tiny pinpoints of heat danced under her skin at the feel of his hard thigh. She hoped fervently that her fingers didn't lock on the wrong object.

Come *on!* she chided herself silently. Be bold. Be a little bawdy. Be Elizabethan. Even with that admonishment, she felt a rush of relief when she located the plastic key. Pulling it out, she fumbled it into the lock.

With the crooked grin that Cari was coming to recognize as Josh Keegan's signature, he shouldered the door open and swept her into the most luxurious suite she'd ever seen. Her eyes rounded as she took in the priceless antiques scattered around a room the size of a football field, the huge bouquets of fresh flowers on every level surface and the wall of windows framing a panoramic view of Atlanta by night.

He set her on her feet. Finally.

Cari spun in a slow circle, as much to catch her breath as to view the gorgeous furnishings. While the woman in her struggled to regain her composure, the historian lost it again at the sight of a beautifully carved Chippendale side chair.

"The pirate trade much be pretty brisk these days," she murmured, eyeing the exquisite piece.

"We do all right," he answered with a careless shrug. Crossing to a Federal-style slant-front desk in dark cherry, he reached for the phone.

More than all right, if he could afford to stay in suites like this one, Cari thought. Golf was obviously a lucrative profession. Golf the way Josh played it, at any rate.

Or had played it.

Cari studied her make-believe groom as he placed an order with room service for champagne and smoked salmon. Did the patch that gave him such a rakish air affect his game? she wondered. Would he continue to play championship golf? She'd heard of athletes overcoming much harsher disabilities than the loss of sight in one eye. She'd seen for herself the incredible achievements of kids with physical limitations during last year's Special Olympics. Was Josh Keegan going back on the pro tour?

An intense curiosity about this tall, broad-shouldered man consumed her, but Cari bit back her questions. Despite the fact that she'd just married him, sort of, she wasn't about to pry into his personal life or ask intimate questions about his physical state.

Josh, it appeared, had no such inhibitions. Folding his arms across his chest, he leaned his hips against the desk and looked her up and down.

"How do you breathe in that thing?" he asked, nodding at her tight bodice.

Her mouth curved. "Very carefully."

"I can't believe women actually strapped themselves into such uncomfortable contraptions." He hooked a brow. "Or did that flat board serve some nefarious purpose, like Queen Juana's balloon skirts?"

"Nothing more nefarious than to exaggerate a woman's charms a bit," Cari admitted, hoping he didn't realize quite how much it exaggerated hers.

"Vanity, thy name is woman," he intoned with a teasing grin.

Cari brushed a hand down her elaborately embroidered bodice. "It is silly, isn't it? Almost as silly as the tight nooses men loop around their necks these days," she added casually. "With lining and stiffening and interfacing, you guys wear fifteen layers of material around your neck every time you put on a tie."

"No kidding? That must be why I never wear the things." He cocked his head, eyeing her elaborate costume. "You seem to know a lot about fashions. Are you in the garment business?"

"In a manner of speaking. I'm a historian, actually. I teach..." She caught herself with a small shake of her head. "I used to teach at Billings College. Now I'm working full-time on my doctoral dissertation."

Cari shoved aside the daunting thought that she wouldn't be working on it for long if the grant she'd applied for didn't come through. She had only six months to finish her thesis. Given the circumstances under which she'd left Billings, there was no way she could expect an extension. With the Atlanta History

Center grant, she'd be able to work night and day and get the finished product in on time. Without it, five years of research might go down the tubes.

She had to eat, after all.

"My thesis deals with the effect of sociological change on modes of dress," she told Josh. "So I guess you could say I'm in the garment business."

"Sounds fascinating," he replied, a corner of his mouth lifting as he surveyed her wide skirts. "When you think about it, Queen Juana was going through a definite sociological change when she invented her hoop."

Cari suspected the lively queen was going to become one of his favorite historical personages. She might have filled him in on more details about the colorful lady, if she hadn't been so distracted by his crooked smile.

Darn it, that grin ought to come with a warning sign. Danger, High Voltage. *Very* High Voltage! Her lips still tingled from the kiss he'd given her downstairs. A kiss she very much hoped he'd offer to repeat.

As if reading her mind, he pushed himself away from the desk and strolled toward her. Cari's stomach did a double back flip as he curled a knuckle under her chin and tilted her face to his.

"Thanks for going along with the gag."

She stared up at him, almost overwhelmed by his sheer, blatant masculinity. He towered over her, his wide shoulders blocking the glow from the lamps. The black patch covering one eye focused all her attention on the other, which danced with golden lights.

A shiver of anticipation darted down her spine, followed immediately by a ripple of nervousness. Common sense told Cari that she was out of her league here. Way out of her league. But a heady recklessness held her still. One more taste, she told herself. One more kiss.

She wet her lips. "As you pointed out, it was for a good cause."

Josh followed the tip of her tongue as it moved over her full, ripe mouth. Without warning, his blood started to pound, and the pulsing ache above his left eye intensified. The pain in his forehead was minor compared to the ache in his lower body, however.

"A very good cause," he murmured, holding her chin steady as he lowered his head. "So is this."

Josh kept this kiss light, unlike the kiss he'd staged for the crowd downstairs. His mouth brushed hers with soft, easy strokes. Her breath was warm and sweet and soon came in quick little puffs. Her lips moved under his, tentatively at first, then with a delicate hunger that sent a sudden, searing pleasure shafting through him.

Josh drew back, startled by the intensity of his body's response. The stunned expression in her wide brown eyes told him she'd been hit by the same unexpected bolt. Her breathless, wide-eyed surprise only added to the urgency pooling in his groin.

Driven by that urgent need, he wrapped an arm around her waist and brought her hard against him. Her breasts swelled against his ribs, and her mouth opened under his. Fitting her against him, Josh plundered its moist richness.

As the explosive kiss went on, he wanted more. Much more. His hand roamed her back, then slipped around to her front, seeking a zipper, or buttons, or whatever the heck held the iron corset together. With a small grunt of satisfaction, he found a row of hooks buried under a flounce of lace. He was breathing hard and fast when she pushed away, her hand fluttering to her upper chest.

"I, uh, don't think my bodice was designed for this kind of activity. I can't seem to catch my breath."

"There's an easy solution to that problem."

Smiling, he reached for the bottom hook. She backed away, eyes wide. A thick strand of hair the color of creamy peanut butter tumbled down to curl around her neck. It lay silky soft against her flushed skin. Josh's stomach corkscrewed into a tight knot at the sight of her swollen lips, red and open and puffing hard.

"This is going a little too fast," she protested breathlessly. "For me, anyway."

The now savage ache over Josh's left eye compounded his searing disappointment at her withdrawal. She was as hot as he was. Hotter, if the tide of red staining her cheeks and neck was any indication. She'd come up to his room willingly enough. Yet now she obviously wanted to be coaxed. Convinced. Or otherwise talked into his bed.

The old Keegan might have accommodated her. The one with the patch over his eye wasn't sure he had the staying power. Not with the pounding pain in his forehead and the tight, hard ache in his loins.

"I'm sorry, sweetheart. I've carried the masquerade this far, but I'm not quite up to playing the ravishing pirate to your outraged captive. Why don't we just get naked and play bride and groom instead?''

It wasn't much of a line, but it was the best Josh could do at the moment. He saw at once that he'd hooked his shot badly and gone out of bounds.

His bride's jaw sagged. She stared at him, open-mouthed, as a host of emotions chased across her expressive face. Josh identified astonishment, indignation and then anger. The color in her cheeks deepened to a bright, flaming red. She drew herself up to her full height, which put the top of her head just about level with his chin.

''No, thank you,'' she said, the ice in her voice a direct contrast to the red flags in her cheeks. ''I think we've carried both masquerades far enough.''

She spun on one heel and tilted crazily, as she had in the ballroom earlier. Josh put out a hand to steady her. She shook it off angrily and marched to the door.

Raking a hand through his hair, Josh winced as even that slight touch added to the pressure inside his skull.

''Cari, wait!'' The words came out sharper than he intended. As did his apology. ''Look, I'm sorry I misread the signals.''

The stain in her cheeks deepened even more, if that was possible. ''Me, too.''

He took a step toward her, only to halt when she flung back her head and flashed him a warning.

''Back off, Keegan. My opinion of men in general isn't all that great these days. And you don't want to know what I think of overmuscled, oversexed jocks in particular at this moment.''

The scorn in her voice nettled Josh. He might have handled her with all the finesse of a Sunday-afternoon duffer trying to hack his way out of the woods, but she'd been a willing participant in the game up to this point. Still, Josh knew when he'd lost a match.

"You're right, I don't particularly want to know," he told her, the hint of sarcasm in his voice inviting her to leave.

She did. With a flounce of her silly hoops and a resounding slam of the door that made Josh wince. His head pounding, he walked into the bedroom and yanked off his shirt.

Cari O'Donnell was just the kind of woman he usually made it a point to avoid, Josh reminded himself in irritation. Obviously she wasn't up to the game as it was played by the pros, and he wasn't ready to play it any other way. Not at this uncertain point in his life, at any rate. His mouth tight, he decided to put the woman and the whole ridiculous evening out of his mind.

At the other end of the long chandeliered corridor, Cari echoed his thoughts exactly.

Josh Keegan, she fumed as she waited for the elevator, was precisely the kind of man any woman with a grain of common sense would avoid like the flu! He was too sure of himself. Too smooth. Too darn handsome and unsettling. Like a virulent virus, he'd raised her blood to fever pitch. Given her the shakes. Left her disoriented. She was lucky she'd gotten out of his hotel room without requiring medical attention!

The elevator doors opened, and Cari swished inside, still fuming. Only now her anger was directed as much at herself as at Keegan. She shook her head in disgust, remembering how she'd melted against the man like a lump of microwaved chocolate.

Melted? Ha! She'd just about puddled around his ankles. Hadn't she learned her lesson with Edward? Did she have to make a fool of herself all over again, this time with a perfect stranger, before she learned to tread warily where men were concerned?

She stepped out of the elevator, anxious to get home and put this whole idiotic night behind her. She needed to regain her equilibrium, to retreat into her research books and a world populated by her beloved Elizabethans. Sir Francis Drake might have been a pirate who lived in a bawdy, freewheeling era, but *he* had class. He wouldn't just invite a woman to get naked and . . .

"Miss O'Donnell?"

The low, musical voice slowed Cari's determined march through the lobby. She turned, recognizing the dark-eyed woman who filled out her black leotards and cat's ears in a way Josh Keegan would certainly have appreciated.

"Yes?"

The woman gave Cari a friendly smile. "I'm Lucy Falco, from Gulliver's Travels. I just wanted to give you your prize."

Cari stared blankly at the envelope the woman held out.

"The donation we matched for charity?" Lucy went on. "The one we converted to a honeymoon cruise for two?"

"This joke has gone far enough. There isn't going to be any honeymoon."

The older woman blinked at the curt reply. "Of course not. But you were a good sport to go along with the whole charade. Here, the prize is yours."

Cari took the thick packet with a mumbled word of thanks. She knew she sounded ungracious, but she was still off balance from her encounter with Atlanta's favorite perennial bachelor. Collecting her velvet cloak from the coat-check room, she swung it around her shoulders, stuffed the prize envelope in a side pocket and hurried out of the hotel.

As she crossed to the adjacent parking lot, a sharp October breeze swirled fallen leaves around her ankles and stole some of the heat from Cari's cheeks. By the time she located her reliable old Buick and worked her farthingale under the steering wheel, she'd regained a measure of her composure.

Only to almost lose it again, as Josh Keegan's face floated before her every time she stopped for a red light. The grainy photos in the tabloids hadn't done him justice, she admitted grudgingly. They certainly hadn't picked up the mahogany lights in his dark hair, or the whiteness of his smile against his tanned skin. Or the way his laughter softened the square, uncompromising line of his jaw.

Her mouth tight, Cari negotiated the Buick through the city streets, then headed south on I-85. Fifteen minutes later, she turned off the interstate and drove through tree-lined streets. Most of the homes in this older, residential area housed faculty and students from Billings College—a good number of whom had been up to some Halloween pranks, Cari soon saw. Toilet-paper streamers decorated several yards, while a straw-stuffed dummy with a startling resemblance to the dean of the business school occupied a chair balanced precariously atop a flagpole just outside the west gate to the campus.

Relieved to see that her apartment complex hadn't suffered anything more than a few smashed pumpkins, Cari parked in her assigned slot. By angling her skirts sideways, she managed to negotiate the stairs to her upper-story apartment.

The cheerful clutter of her home welcomed her like an old friend. Over the years, Cari had spent far more on books than on furniture. They spilled out of the wall-to-wall bookshelves, vying for space with the jumble of green plants that Cari nurtured like children. More stacks of books and potted plants made an obstacle course out of her living room floor. Another tall pile sat beside a feathery fern on her roll-top desk, which constituted the only piece of furniture in the room, apart from a comfortable, well-worn sofa. Colorful prints from the Museum of History and Science decorated the off-white walls, along with an ornately framed portrait of an early Dutch settler that Cari had picked up at a garage sale. She blew him a kiss as she weaved her way through the stacks to her bedroom.

"Hello, Van Dyke."

Shrugging out of her cloak, she reached in the closet for a hanger. Only then did she remember the envelope stuffed in its pocket. She dug through the velvet folds and pulled out the thick packet. Curious, she riffled through the contents, then extracted a glossy brochure. Her breath caught in sheer delight at the picture on the front.

A gleaming white yacht. A sparkling aquamarine bay. Tall palms fringing a curving shore.

Opening the brochure, she skimmed the bold print. Nassau. Saint Thomas. Grand Cayman Island. Cancún. A ten-day cruise, exploring the splendors of the past while cradled in every luxury the present could offer.

Intrigued, she read on. Old forts. Sunken treasure. Ancient Mayan pyramids. A select group of ten passengers. An experienced captain and crew, one of whom was a world-class chef.

The perfect honeymoon for a history buff, Cari thought with a small smile. If she'd planned the trip herself, she couldn't have come up with a more idyllic itinerary. Sighing, she flipped the brochure over and skimmed the departure dates.

The next cruise left from Miami tomorrow afternoon.

Cari stared at the date for several long moments, then shook her head. No! No way! She couldn't afford a cruise like this, unless the prize package covered every major expense.

Did it?

Curious, she dug through envelope once more. Good grief, it did. Even the taxi fare from Miami airport to where the yacht was docked.

Oh, for heaven's sake! Assuming there was still cabin space available, she couldn't just take off for ten days. Not at this uncertain juncture in her life. Tossing the brochure on the antique chest that served as a nightstand, she reached for the drawstring of her heavy skirt.

Why couldn't she?

The wayward thought stilled her fingers. She wouldn't hear about the grant until the end of next week. If she got it, she wouldn't come up for air, much less take a vacation, for the next six months. If she didn't, she'd be pounding the streets looking for short-term work while she circulated her résumé.

No! She was nuts to even consider it. She had too much work to do on her thesis, too many uncertainties in her life right now, to go cruising through the Caribbean.

Three

Josh woke to a sunshine-filled room and a blessed absence of pain. Lacing his hands behind his head, he enjoyed both. Gradually memories of the night before filtered through his lazy contentment.

He'd pulled a few crazy stunts in his time, for charity, for publicity, and occasionally just for laughs and to release the intense pressures that built up on the tour. Once, he and a left-handed competitor had switched clubs on a bet and kept the gallery hooting with laughter during a wild practice round. Early in his rookie days, Josh had shown up for a tournament hosted by "friends of the environment." They'd been friendly, all right. The friendliest nudists Josh had ever played a round of golf with. He'd gotten burned that day on parts of his body that rarely saw the sun.

But last night's escapade ranked right up there

among his crazier stunts. In the bright light of day, he had a hard time believing he'd actually exchanged phony marriage vows with a complete stranger in front of a ballroom full of partygoers.

Although...

For a while last night, it had appeared that the gag would lead to some unexpected fringe benefits. His bride had the softest, fullest, sweetest mouth Josh had tasted in a long time. Come to think of it, he couldn't remember ever experiencing such an instantaneous, explosive reaction to a kiss.

The image of Cari O'Donnell's expressive eyes and wide, generous mouth teased at Josh, banishing his early-morning lethargy. One by one, his muscles tensed. An echo of the desire that had gripped him last night threaded through his veins.

Josh frowned, wondering just what it was about Cari that had gotten under his skin like this. Sure, her tawny hair, creamy skin and huge brown eyes would snare any man's interest. Despite her piquant appeal, however, this particular woman came complete with a bundle of feminine contradictions that confused the hell out of him.

She'd rigged herself out in a costume that displayed most of her upper deck, yet she'd blushed like a schoolgirl when his appreciative gaze lingered on the view. For all her initial reluctance to participate in the mock ceremony, she'd been willing enough to come up to his room for a private postwedding celebration. What was more, she'd tumbled into his arms with an eagerness that set Josh's blood pounding, then pushed herself away and laid into him with a few scathing words.

He grimaced at the memory. Oversexed, overmuscled jock that he was, he'd obviously made a few wrong assumptions about Cari, but he was damned if he knew what they were.

He shook his head, deciding to put her and the whole incident out of his mind. He had more important matters to concern him at this point in his life. Like earning a living.

Flinging aside the sheets, he called room service for a light breakfast, then padded naked to the bathroom. While he waited for the shower to heat, he reviewed the game plan he'd laid out last night.

First he'd call Walt Henshaw, his longtime trainer, to set up a session at the country club where Walt worked as PGA pro.

Next he'd check out of the hotel and get his butt home to collect his gear. He'd stayed here last night only because his vision wasn't reliable enough for night driving. He could be at the club within an hour, two at most.

Then he'd start swinging a club again. It was time—past time!—he learned to connect a club face with a ball while wearing a patch over one eye. The doctors gave him fifty-fifty odds on regaining full sight, but Josh couldn't wait around for the dice to roll. If he laid off his game much longer, he'd lose both his rhythm and his competitive edge.

Stepping into the steamy shower, he lifted his face to the hot, stinging pellets. Fierce determination surged through him, as strong as any he'd felt during his years on the circuit. He itched to hold a club in his hands again and hear the satisfying crack of a ball solidly hit.

He'd just stepped out of the shower and pulled on a thick terry robe with the hotel's logo on the pocket when a sharp rap on the door to his suite heralded the arrival of his breakfast. Impatient now to get started on his agenda, Josh belted the robe and strode into the sitting room.

"Morning, Mr. Keegan."

"Good morning."

A tall, gangly youth in a maroon waiter's jacket deposited a silver tray containing a coffee carafe, a basket of rolls and a neatly folded newspaper on the table by the window. Josh took the pen he offered, added a hefty tip to the total and scribbled his name across the bill.

The waiter pocketed the ticket, then hesitated. "Would you mind signing your name again? As an autograph, I mean. My dad's a big fan of yours. He still talks about your two-iron shot to the green during the U.S. Open three years ago. He'll have a bird if I bring home your autograph."

"Better he has a birdie," Josh replied with an easy grin as he turned over a paper napkin. "What's his name?"

The door closed behind the beaming waiter a few moments later. Josh poured himself a cup of coffee and flipped open the morning edition of the *Atlanta Constitution*. When he spotted the picture in the lower left-hand corner of the third page, he choked on a gulp of coffee. Swallowing hastily, Josh stared at the grainy shot.

A bleary-eyed judge with an old-fashioned wig dangling precariously on one side of his head glared back at him. Setting aside his coffee cup, Josh picked up the paper and read the caption under the picture.

Retired state supreme court justice Benjamin Tyce III was arrested after driving his vehicle through the front window of Comet Laundry and Dry Cleaning. When charged with driving under the influence, Justice Tyce announced that he'd stopped by to pick up his shirts.

"I'll be damned. The little guy was for real."

Grinning, Josh flipped to page twelve to read the accompanying story. When he got to the last paragraph, his grin slipped.

Judge Tyce protested his arrest, citing an obscure statute enacted more than a century ago that grants supreme court judges extraordinary powers. The district attorney is confident the DUI charges will stand, however. His office plans to issue a statement later today concerning the disposition of the case.

Eyes narrowing, Josh skimmed the short paragraph again. Obscure act? Extraordinary powers? The first tendrils of unease curled in his chest.

What the heck was the phrase the judge used last night? Plenipotentiary powers? Everyone, Josh included, had assumed he'd pulled it out of his hat as part of the joke. Maybe... maybe it wasn't a joke.

His unease sharpening to a deep foreboding, Josh strode to the desk, staring at the paper fisted in one hand. Yanking up the phone, he punched in his long-time friend's number.

When Harry came on the line, Josh gave him a succinct summary of the newspaper article, liberally interspersed with acidic comments about his friend's harebrained ideas. Then he held the receiver away from his ear while the lawyer whooped with laughter.

"If you're through," he asked icily when Harry's bull-like hoots had dwindled to devilish cackles, "you might just tell me if there's any possibility the ceremony was really legal."

"It's possible," the lawyer replied between snickers. "We still have all kinds of archaic statutes on the books that have never been repealed. Did you know it's against the law to tie your horse to a hitching post on the left side of the street on Sundays? I think that one has something to do with giving the street sweeper a break so he could attend church services."

Josh ground his teeth and suggested a few places Harry could tie his horse. That set his friend off again.

"This is priceless," Harry wheezed some moments later. "Absolutely priceless. Wait till I call Joan."

"Oh, right! All I need is for the programming chief of CNN news to hear about this!"

"C'mon, Josh. She's my wife. Aside from the fact that she's been after you for years to give up your philandering ways, she'll kill me if someone else scoops the story."

"I'm going to kill you if *anyone* scoops this story." Josh drew in a deep breath. "Give me a break here, Harry. The hoopla from the accident has finally died down. I want to start swinging a club again, and I

can't do it with a pack of photographers and camera-
men recording and analyzing every shot I miss."

The merriment left his friend's voice instantly.
Harry was one of the few people who'd witnessed the
disastrous results the few times Josh had tried to hit a
ball since the accident.

"Let me check into this, buddy. You'd better give
me the phone number for your, ah, wife. In case I
need to contact her. What was her name?"

"Caren O'Donnell," Josh answered tightly. "She
goes by Cari. I don't have her number."

"What? We all saw you carry her out of the ballroom and head for the elevators. Don't tell me you
duffed your shot with her?"

"Big-time."

"Oh-oh. Well, see if you can track her down while
I check out the judge's exact legal powers." Harry
hesitated. "She's probably read the newspaper story
by now. We might have to do a little damage control
here, pal."

"What are you talking about?"

"Look, I specialize in corporate tax shelters, not
divorces. But it might not be as easy to get you out of
this marriage as it was to get you into it. If it turns out
you're really married, our best bet is to resolve the
matter quickly, before your wife—"

"Will you stop with the wife business!"

"Before *Ms. O'Donnell* starts thinking about things
like community property and alimony."

If she did, Josh thought cynically as he hung up a
few moments later, she was in for a rude awakening.
Two very expensive eye surgeries and their attendant
medical expenses had eaten a big chunk out of his well-

publicized winnings. Given his questionable future on the pro tour at this point, Josh couldn't count on any income from that source. Sure, he had plenty of offers from sports equipment companies, begging him to endorse their products, but he wasn't any more ready to make a full-time career out of hustling golf shoes than he was chairing charity events.

Dammit, he didn't need a complication like this! Not now. Not when he'd decided to try to get his game going again.

Simmering with frustration, he yanked open the desk drawer and hefted out the white pages. He might as well track Cari down and arrange to meet her this afternoon—in Harry's presence.

He didn't find a listing for Caren or Cari O'Donnell in the Atlanta directory, but he did find seventeen C. O'Donnells. Swearing, Josh started dialing.

Eleven answering machines, four wrong numbers, one hang-up and one disconnected line later, he was no closer to finding his prey. He hadn't recognized any of the voices on the answering machines. He could only assume that Cari had arranged for a male friend to make the recording to disguise the fact she lived alone. Either that, or she lived outside the Atlanta area.

He drummed his fingers on the desk, dredging his memory for the few snatches of conversation they'd had. She taught history, he recalled. At...where the heck was it? Billings!

Within moments, he had the chairman of the history department on the line. Dr. Edward Grant hesitated at first to discuss his former colleague, but Josh knew how to apply the good-ol'-boy conversational grease. The somewhat pompous professor soon unbent and provided a sketchy, rather disturbing background on Caren O'Donnell.

According to Grant, she was a brilliant researcher, but regrettably impulsive. She'd left Billings under questionable circumstances a few months ago and, as far as anyone knew, was currently unemployed.

"Great," Josh muttered as he hung up. "Just great."

Harry's warning about alimony and community property clanged like a siren in his mind. Cari hadn't struck him as the gold-digger type, but Josh had sure misread a few other signals concerning her last night. With a sinking sensation, he realized that this mess could soon get a whole lot messier.

He'd wait till he heard something definitive from Harry, he decided, then track Cari down at the address he'd wormed out of Grant. One way or another, he'd get this matter straightened out quickly, then get on with his life.

Two hours later, Josh was aiming his two seater convertible south on I-85 and fighting the urge to stomp the accelerator to the floor. Of all the farcical, idiotic, asinine situations!

He was legally married! To a woman he'd exchanged a half-dozen sentences with. A dozen, at most. Well, he'd soon exchange a few more...while he hustled his *wife* to the lawyer Harry had recommended, to arrange a very quick and very quiet divorce.

Gripping the steering wheel with white-knuckled fists, Josh exited the interstate and drove through streets lined with towering oaks and waxy-leaved magnolias. He found the small apartment complex he was looking for with little difficulty.

A petite gray-haired woman with a watering can in one wrinkled hand answered his knock. A hint of wariness crossed the woman's face when she took in his grim expression. And his eye patch.

"Yes?"

Josh couldn't do anything about the patch, but he did manage to crank up a grin. "I'm looking for Caren O'Donnell. I was told she lived at this address."

His smile eased some of her stiffness. "She does."

"I'm sorry to barge in on you like this, Ms.—?"

"Mrs. Wilder. I'm Cari's neighbor."

"Is Cari home?"

Despite her tentative answering smile, the woman remained cautious. "Are you a friend? Or relative?"

Josh debated how to answer that one, and finally settled on friend. "My name's Josh Keegan," he added, pulling a card out of his wallet to confirm his identity.

Mrs. Wilder's pale blue eyes rounded. "Josh Keegan? The golfer? I read about you in *Daytime Digest* last month, you and Jessica Hope— Oh!" She clapped a hand over her mouth. "That's ended, isn't it?"

It had never really begun, but neither Josh nor the glamorous star of a popular daytime soap had been able to convince the media of that.

"Yes, it's over. Is Cari home? I'd like to speak to her."

Josh glanced over the neighbor's shoulder, frowning as he surveyed what looked like a cross between a tropical rain forest and a public library. If there was any furniture in the place, he couldn't see it.

Wonderful! His— Josh choked. His *wife* was out of work, and apparently possessed few visible assets. Harry's gloomy prognostications on what it might cost to extricate himself from this mess were beginning to look like very real possibilities. Josh dragged his attention back to Mrs. Wilder, who was now bubbling over with eagerness to help.

"No, Cari's not home. She called me early this morning, all excited about a vacation she'd won."

"A vacation?"

"Some kind of cruise or something. She had to leave right away to catch the boat, and asked me to water her plants."

Ten minutes later, Josh peeled back onto I-85 and pointed the low-slung convertible north.

Dammit to hell, this was turning into a first-class goat rope! He couldn't quite believe a half-size pansy-eyed female he didn't even know was turning his whole life upside down.

After a brief stop at Gulliver's Travels, he screeched into the parking lot of an office complex done in mellow brick and wrought iron reminiscent of Atlanta's past. Pulling into the slot reserved for Harry's partner, he slammed the car door and stalked into the law offices. A startled receptionist quickly showed him into the walnut-paneled inner sanctum.

Harry listened to Josh's scathing status report, chewing on his lower lip thoughtfully.

"This cruise could be a real break for our side," he said when Josh had finished. "If she left as early this morning as her landlady said, she might not have seen the paper."

"So?"

"So you catch up with her," Harry urged. "Take her by surprise. Get her written agreement to a quickie divorce the moment she returns from the cruise." His eyes lit up. "Or better yet, before she returns. Have you got a copy of the itinerary?"

Josh tossed the package he'd picked up from the travel agency on the table. Harry dug through it and scanned a glossy pamphlet.

"All right! The boat docks at Cancún seven days from now. We'll set up a nice, quick Mexican divorce."

"Wait a minute...."

"It'll work, Josh. Trust me. I'll get in touch with an associate of mine who specializes in divorces and have him set up everything from this end. All you have to do is waltz your wife—" he caught Josh's scowl "—er, waltz Miss O'Donnell in and out of the registry office before she has a chance to change her mind."

"Are you sure a Mexican divorce is recognized in the U.S.?"

"The law varies from state to state. I'll have to double-check on Georgia, but I'm almost certain we're okay on this."

"Almost certain?"

"I'll check on it," Harry promised again.

His scowl deepening, Josh shoved a hand through his hair. "I don't like it."

"Why not?"

"It doesn't feel right."

"Oh, sure. And being married to a perfect stranger does?"

Josh didn't have any answer for that one.

"Go home," Harry urged. "Throw some things in a bag. Catch up with your missing bride tomorrow in ... Where does the boat dock first? In Nassau. Explain the situation and get her agreement. You two will be divorced before she really grasps the fact that you're married."

Cari bent one leg and languorously stretched both arms above her head. Heat pulsed down on her bare limbs.

A distant, lazy corner of her mind acknowledged that the lingering effects of this fierce tropical sun might kill her twenty or thirty years from now. And when she tried to stand up, she'd probably regret slurping down the rainbow of rum and fruit juices the steward had mixed for her when she returned to the ship awhile ago. At this moment, she couldn't bring herself to worry about either eventuality.

For the first time in months, she was totally, bonelessly relaxed. She didn't even have a book in her hands! It lay on the polished teak deck beside her lounge chair, lost amid the clutter of tanning oil, terrycloth cover-up, and sunglasses. She lifted her face to the sun, glorying in its heat.

She still couldn't quite believe she was here! Lounging on the upper deck of a private yacht that Aristotle Onassis might have lusted for! Or that she'd soon make her way downstairs to a stateroom twice the size of her apartment to prepare for dinner. She'd felt a twinge of guilt when she was shown to what the captain jokingly called the honeymoon suite, but she'd gotten over that when he explained it was the only cabin available.

Wide-eyed, she'd explored the unbelievably luxurious quarters. The two-room suite was all gleaming brass and teak fittings. Acres of pale champagne-colored satin on a bed the size of Rhode Island. A bar stocked with labels like Courvoisier and Glenlivet. A whirlpool tub that would seat three and sleep two comfortably. A cedar-lined closet that swallowed up Cari's few clothes.

Thank goodness she'd flung her only decent cocktail dress into her suitcase yesterday morning, along with a hastily assembled assortment of shorts and sundresses, the bathing suit she rarely wore, and a dozen or so research volumes. As she'd discovered last night, one dressed for dinner aboard the *Nautilus III*.

One dressed for everything aboard the *Nautilus III*!

The array of diamond rings and silk ascots and white linen suits that greeted Cari when she rushed up the gangplank minutes before departure yesterday afternoon had intimidated her just a bit. Nor had it helped her composure to find herself seated across from the only other single aboard at dinner last night—a thirteen-year-old wearing pleated white pants, a superbly cut navy blazer and a gold ring in his left nostril. Although his grandparents were delightful, the kid had a definite attitude. When his grandparents could get him to talk at all, he mostly just groused about spending his boarding school break on a ten-day cruise with them instead of joining his buddies at a soccer clinic.

Eric's surliness at dinner had put only a small dent in Cari's enjoyment of the cruise, however. So far, it had been a voyage of discovery. Yesterday, she'd enjoyed the thrill of watching the sun sink into silvery sea and dining under a canopy of stars.

And today! Today, she'd strolled the narrow, teeming streets of Nassau, capital city of the Bahamas. Given her limited funds, Cari had avoided the glittering import shops on the main thoroughfare. Instead, she'd spent a wonderful morning getting lost in side streets lined with pretty old pastel homes. The highlights of her afternoon had been visits to Fort Montagu and Blackbeard's Tower, a mossy old ruin said to have been erected by the pirate Edward Teach.

She stretched again, grimacing a bit as thoughts of another pirate drifted through her mind. Blackbeard didn't have anything on Josh Keegan when it came to carrying women off to have their way with them, she decided. Resolutely she ignored a sharp twinge of regret that she hadn't let him. Have his way with her, that is.

Come on, O'Donnell, she admonished herself. This is the nineties. No one with a lick of sense indulges in casual affairs or one-night stands anymore. Not that she had ever indulged in either, she admitted with a small sigh. She'd saved herself. For Edward.

Wrinkling her nose at that humongous mistake, Cari shoved all thought of men and sex out of her mind. She had nine more days of unimaginable luxury and sun-kissed islands ahead of her. She'd explore exotic ports. Sip colorful rum drinks. Feast on the gourmet meals prepared by the yacht's chef. And sleep in the sun, storing up energy for the grind that would greet her when she got back to Atlanta.

She had just drifted into a doze when a deep voice suddenly growled at her.

"Miss O'Donnell?"

Holding up a hand to shield her eyes from the red ball of the sun, Cari squinted at a blurry silhouette. Enrique. That was his name. The chief steward. The only man aboard with shoulders that size. He'd brought her that wonderful drink earlier, and promised to show her how to work his pride and joy, the high-tech digitized massage device in the fantastically equipped spa. Cari wasn't into exercise, but a body massage sounded heavenly.

"Hi, Enrique. Ready to go below and show me how to get loose?"

She reached for her terry-cloth robe and stood, expecting him to move aside and give her room. Instead, he loomed over her like a towering stone monolith.

Startled, Cari backed away—or tried to.

The edge of the lounge chair hit her calves, and she plopped down again. Shielding her eyes with the back of her hand, she squinted up at the figure above her. Only then did she realize that he wasn't wearing the white slacks and discreetly monogrammed shirt of a crew member. Surprised, she took in tan twill slacks and a red knit polo shirt. Surprise spiraled into a squeak of astonishment when she crooked her neck back and saw the tanned face glowering down at her.

"Wh-what are you doing here?"

Josh fisted both hands at his sides as he struggled with wildly conflicting emotions. After a hectic twenty-four hours, he'd finally caught up with his bride. The last time he saw her, she'd been laced into an iron corset that displayed as much as it concealed. Her hair had been puffed away from her face, giving her delicate features a regal air that matched her costume. She'd looked intriguing, and sexy as hell.

Now she wore a demure, old-fashioned bathing suit that covered far more than it revealed. Long bangs and layers of windblown buckskin hair all but obscured a mouth wiped clean of color, a nose slathered with greasy sunscreen and brown eyes rounded in amazement. She looked disconcerted and dismayed. And sexy as hell.

Josh hadn't expected the attraction that slammed into him the moment he spotted Cari stretched out in the deck chair like a sleek, lazy cat. Any more than he'd anticipated this fierce, unreasoning anger at the idea of her getting loose...with anyone!

"Who's Enrique?"

She blinked at the whiplike question. "The steward. How did you get here? *Why* are you here?"

The steward? Josh shook his head, suspecting that he might have jumped to the wrong conclusion. Maybe. What the hell was it about this woman that threw him off stride every time he tangled with her? A dull throb started just above his left eye.

"I'm here because we have to talk."

At his terse reply, she scrambled off the far side of the deck chair. Clutching a terry robe to her chest with both fists, she stared at him.

"Talk about what? Is something wrong?"

Josh glanced around the polished deck. A hulking dark-haired crewman in pristine white slacks watched them curiously from a few feet away. Enrique, no doubt.

"Couldn't they collect the pledges?"

Cari's worried voice dragged Josh's attention back to her face. Under the fringe of feathery bangs, her eyes had widened to huge pools of chocolate. When he didn't reply immediately, alarm chased across her expressive features.

"Oh, no! They're not trying to hold us responsible for the ten thousand, are they? I don't have it. I don't have half of it!"

Harry's dire predictions rang in Josh's ears like deep, booming gongs. He closed his eye, took a slow breath and ignored the sharp stab of pain in his forehead.

"Why don't we go below? So we can talk. Privately."

Four

"**M**arried?"

Cari's shriek bounced off the green marble wall panels of her cabin. Shock pounded through her veins, followed instantly by disbelief.

"I can't be married! Not to you!"

The sardonic lift of his brow told Cari that she'd been less than tactful, but she was too stunned to care.

"Look, it's nothing personal. I don't want to be married to anyone. Not for the next hundred years or so, at least."

He made no response to that, except to lean his hips against the back of the jade-green leather sofa. Shoving his hands in his pockets, he watched her with narrowed eyes. Eye.

"Are you sure the ceremony was legal?" she demanded, still disbelieving. "The judge was pretty tipsy. And we didn't sign anything."

"It was legal, according to two of Atlanta's most expensive lawyers."

"Expensive lawyers? Oh, God!"

Spinning on one heel, Cari paced the spacious cabin. Her bare feet sank into plush champagne-colored carpet with each agitated step.

"I can't afford expensive lawyers. I can't afford any kind of lawyers right now. I can't even afford plant food until I hear about the..."

A horrifying thought struck her. Whirling, she faced her... her *husband!*

"How much do you make a year?"

He didn't move, didn't alter his casual stance by so much as a flutter of an eyelid. But a steel mask seemed to descend over his face. His jaw, already square, took on rigid ninety-degree angles. He gave her a look that would have sliced right through her if she hadn't been so distracted by the awful, sinking sensation in the pit of her stomach.

"Why?"

Thinking of all those tabloid headlines, she barely heard the ice in his voice. "It's a lot, isn't it?"

The tight look on his face confirmed her worst fears.

"More than a lot," she groaned. "Gazillions."

"Not quite," he replied in a slow, dangerous drawl.

She resumed her frantic pacing. "I'm dead! They're going to think I lied. That I falsified the financial data on my application."

"What application?"

"I'm dead!" she repeated, taking another distraught turn. "If anyone finds out we're married, I can forget about the grant. Forget about finishing my disserta—"

Two hard hands caught her forearms and brought her up short. "What the hell are you talking about?"

"My grant!" she wailed.

A gold-flecked eye bored into her. "What grant?"

"I applied for financial assistance from the Atlanta History Center. To finish my dissertation. The award is based on merit and on need. I won't qualify if my income or—" she stumbled over the next words "—or my *spouse's* income exceeds the basic minimum."

He stared down at her, a muscle ticking in one side of his jaw. Cari ignored his obvious tension as she fought to master her swamping dismay.

If she didn't get the grant, there was no way she could finish her dissertation on time. In their last, turbulent meeting, Edward had warned her that she wouldn't get an extension. Not with him chairing the department.

The jerk!

The hard grip on her arms dragged her thoughts from the recent past to the immediate present. She stared up at Josh's taut face, searching for a way out of this unexpected dilemma.

"Maybe we can get an annulment," she suggested in desperation. "Or do you have to be Catholic for that?"

"I have no idea."

Her fingers curled into the front of his red knit polo shirt. "I know! Your friend, Billy Bob! He could push a special bill through the legislature, invalidating that ridiculous law.''

"Cari..."

"He'd have to do it fast. The grant committee meets next week. On Friday, I think. You could call him. Right now."

"Listen to me, Cari. There's an easier way. We can get a divorce."

Her whirling thoughts came to a sudden and complete halt. "A...divorce?"

He nodded. "In Cancún, when the ship docks there, early next week."

Later, Cari would realize that her instinctive reaction sprang from her heart and not her head. At the moment, however, all she could do was gulp as distaste curdled like sour milk in her stomach. The word echoed hollowly in her mind.

Divorce.

She'd be divorced.

Before she'd really been married.

The thought depressed her to the depths of her hopelessly romantic soul. The idea of a divorce tromped all over her somewhat dented illusions about love and weddings and marriages that lasted a lifetime. She clutched at the red knit shirt and fought the most idiotic urge to cry.

Watching the play of emotions on the face so close to his own, Josh bit back a curse. Not two minutes ago, he'd been sure Harry's worst predictions were about to come true. Now, he wasn't sure of anything, least of all his sudden, compulsive urge to wrap his arms around Cari and cradle her against his chest. Even with the lancing ache in his skull that darkened the edges of his vision, he hadn't missed her dismay. Or the bright sheen of tears that now filled her eyes.

Blinking furiously, she stepped out of his hold. Josh's arms dropped to his side.

"Sorry," she murmured, flags of embarrassment riding high in her cheeks. "I don't know why, but divorce sounds so...so ugly and traumatic."

"It doesn't have to be ugly. Or traumatic. Not if it's quick."

"Right. Quick and painless." She managed a strained smile. "Like our marriage."

"Right."

Shoving her hands into the pockets of her terrycloth cover-up, she hunched her shoulders. "So, uh, how do we go about this?"

"Harry... You met him the other night. He was the one in horns and a pointed tail."

"I remember."

"He's arranging everything through an associate with contacts in Mexico."

"Won't we need passports? Or a marriage certificate?"

"Harry drafted a document detailing the validity of the marriage. He was going to get the judge's signature when I left this morning. He promised to fax the document to me as soon as it was signed and notarized."

"And that's all we'll need?"

"According to Harry's associate."

"Oh. Well, we're all set, then."

Josh drew in a slow breath. "Almost. We have to file for the divorce a minimum of five days before the hearing. Harry got the forms from the Mexican consulate. The sooner we sign them and get them off, the better.''

She nodded, and Josh wondered why the hell he felt so guilty at her ready acquiescence. She wanted the divorce as badly as he did. Digging into his back pocket, he extracted a set of folded papers.

''Here, why don't you look them over while I find the captain and arrange for a cabin?''

Her brows disappeared into the fringe of her feathery bangs. ''A cabin? You're joining the cruise?''

''Is that a problem?''

''No, not a problem,'' she replied, mastering her surprise with a visible effort. ''I just assumed we'd meet a week from now, in Cancún.''

Josh would have preferred to do exactly that. Get her signature on the forms and meet her in Mexico to do the deed. But a week was a long time. Given what he'd learned of Cari's impulsive nature, there was no telling what she might do in the course of a week. Like change her mind. Or talk to the wrong people. Or otherwise foul up what Harry assured him would be an easy process. No, both Harry and his associate had agreed it would be better if Josh stuck close to her until the boat docked in Cancún.

He passed her the forms. ''Here, look these over. We can talk about them later, after I get settled.''

He left her standing in the center of the cabin, staring at the blank forms.

He was back below decks some fifteen minutes later, his leather hang-up in one hand and a crumpled fax in the other. Jaws tight, he rapped his knuckles on the polished teak door.

Dammit! This whole situation was rapidly sliding from the farcical into the absurd.

He rapped again, harder. When Cari didn't answer, he inserted the key the captain had presented him with just moments ago and stepped inside. The steady drum of a shower explained why she hadn't heard his knock.

Tossing his hang-up and the fax onto the leather sofa, Josh crossed a half acre of pale carpet to the wet bar built into the starboard bulkhead. He ignored the impressive array of premium labels and splashed two fingers of tap water into a heavy cut-crystal snifter. Digging in his pants pocket, he extracted his prescription painkillers. As much as he hated to take the damned things, he wasn't about to let the ache in his forehead blossom into full-fledged, sledge-driving pain. Not until he explained the latest development in their on-again, off-again marriage to... He gulped down the pills. To his wife.

While he waited for the pills to work and for Cari to emerge from the bathroom, Josh surveyed the opulent suite. Concerned only with Cari's reaction to his news, he'd noted few details before. He now saw that the lavish stateroom extended the full width of the yacht. A huge bed awash in a sea of pale gold satin dominated one half of the room. The other half served as a living room, with the jade leather sofa and matching easy chairs grouped around a massive oak and brass coffee table. A sophisticated high-tech entertainment system took up a good portion of the rear bulkhead. To the right of that, sliding glass doors gave onto a small private deck with a breathtaking vista of the turquoise bay beyond.

Josh had sailed aboard luxurious private yachts before. He'd spent a weekend cruising the California coast with a group put together by a well-known movie star who also happened to be a golf addict. He'd angled for marlin several times off the Florida Keys with a sporting-goods magnate. Once, he'd joined the U.S. President for dinner aboard the *Sequoia* after a pro-am charity event in Washington. But the *Nautilus III* outclassed all the other boats, even the presidential yacht.

Idly Josh wondered how Gulliver's Travels could afford to donate a prize package that included a cruise aboard a boat like this, even at a substantial discount. From what he'd seen of the travel agency during his hasty visit yesterday, it carried on a brisk trade, but still...

His gaze fell on a set of folded papers on the desk in one corner of the sitting area. Frowning, he crossed the length of the stateroom and unfolded the wrinkled sheets.

She'd signed the divorce petition. With no discussion. No arguments. No demands.

Josh waited for the rush of relief that should have come with the sight of her signature, but all he felt was a strange dissatisfaction with the whole damned business. And a curious sense of anticipation. For the first time since the accident, an echo of his former vitality hummed in his veins. The eagerness reflected his decision to get on with his life, Josh knew. As soon as this business with Cari was settled, he'd follow through on the agenda he'd outlined yesterday morning.

By the time the sound of running water ceased, the painkiller had done its work. In control once again, Josh waited for his soon-to-be-ex to appear.

She strolled through the door a few moments later, her head buried in a thick white towel and her body wrapped in another. The wide band of white around her middle covered more of her trim figure than the blue-striped swimsuit had, but it covered her...differently.

Less demurely.

More precariously.

It took Josh a moment to realize that the sudden, furious pounding in his forehead had nothing to do with his eye injury. A whole lot more than vitality hummed through his veins at the sight of the moisture beaded on her shoulders. He had the craziest urge to lick those dewdrops from her skin, one by one. He cleared his throat, more noisily than he'd intended.

Cari jumped half out of her towels.

Josh's heart jumped all the way out of his chest and lodged in the vicinity of his Adam's apple.

Yanking the towel off her wet, tangled hair, she held it in front of her and shot him a fierce glare. "Listen here, Keegan! We may be sort of married, but that doesn't give you unlimited conjugal visitation rights. How about knocking the next time you—"

She broke off, her glare tipping into a ferocious scowl. "Wait a minute. I'm sure I locked the door before I got in the shower. How did you get in?"

"With a key."

"A key? Where did you get a key?"

"The captain gave it to me. Right when he handed me the fax Harry's secretary sent through the on-board communications link."

She tilted her head, dangling a mass of wet wheat-colored hair over one shoulder. "I'm missing something here. Why would—?" Her brown eyes widened as comprehension dawned. "Oh, no!"

"Oh, yes," Josh confirmed. "The captain had read the fax and found out about the recent ceremony. He offered his heartiest congratulations, by the way."

"He thinks we're really married?" she squeaked.

"We are married," Josh reminded her. Then he dropped the next bombshell. "Unfortunately, a few of the passengers overheard our conversation."

"Oh, no. Does everyone on the boat think we're married?"

"We are married."

"Stop saying that!" She drew in a steadying breath. "What did they say when you told them we were on our way to a divorce?"

"Well..."

She peered at him suspiciously. "You did tell them, didn't you?"

"No."

"Why not?"

Josh shoved a hand through his hair. "It gets complicated."

Cari groaned. "Do I want to hear this?"

Despite his own disgust with the latest turn of events, Josh felt a grin tug at his lips. "Probably not."

She plopped down on the edge of the bed, towel still clutched in both hands. "Tell me."

"If word of our marriage or divorce leaks, the media will swarm all over us like blood-starved mosquitoes. We'll have boatloads of reporters following the *Nautilus*, and news helicopters buzzing us day and night. We wouldn't have a moment of privacy or peace during the entire cruise. Nor would anyone else aboard the *Nautilus III*."

"Oh, wonderful."

"The only way I could think of to avoid a media plague was to let the captain and the passengers think we were on our honeymoon and ask them to respect our privacy."

Dismay filled her face. "They all think we're on our honeymoon?"

"Well, we are."

Her mouth opened. Snapped shut. Opened again.

"Look, I'm not any happier than you are about this ridiculous situation," Josh told her.

She raked a hand through wet, tangled hair, leaving a crown of spiked bangs above her forehead. Josh waited in mounting anticipation to hear what she'd say about the latest installment in their continuing soap opera.

"I'm getting a little dizzy," she said at last. "In the space of twenty minutes, I've gone from wife to divorced woman to honeymooner. Just out of curiosity, when do I go back to being unattached again?"

"In Cancún, as planned. If we can keep everything under wraps till then, we might be able to get out of this mess relatively unscathed. Until then, though, you're stuck with me." He glanced around the cabin. "Literally."

She let out an indignant squawk. "Wait a minute! Sharing a cabin wasn't part of the deal. Not that there ever *was* a deal, but that definitely wasn't part of it."

Josh shrugged. "Can you think of a logical reason for honeymooners to occupy separate cabins?"

She chewed on her lower lip, obviously unhappy, but unable to come up with another alternative.

"All right," she conceded, with something less than graciousness. "But I was here first. I get the bed. You can take the couch."

Josh couldn't help himself. She looked so put out and prissy-prim, despite her spiked hair and near-naked state. Slipping into a familiar role, he smiled lazily.

"It's a big bed. Sure you don't want to share?"

He watched in amusement as a tide of pink rose from her shoulders to her neck to her cheeks. She couldn't hide her emotions if she wore a golf bag over her head. As he'd learned the night he met her, however, embarrassment didn't blunt her ability to lay things on the line.

"Let's get one thing straight. Married or not, I don't intend to...to get naked and play bride and groom with you."

"Fair enough." His half smile deepened to a wicked grin. "And I'll try not to play ravishing pirate to your outraged captive."

The pink in her cheeks flared into red. "Try hard, Mr. Keegan. *Very* hard!"

"We're on our honeymoon, remember? Don't you think you should call me Josh?"

"I can think of several things I'd like to call you," she muttered. She chewed on her lip a moment longer.

then leveled him a straight look. "This situation is difficult enough as it is. Please, don't make it worse by turning on the playboy charm. I'm not in your league. I don't know how to handle it...or you."

"I'd say you handle both pretty well," he replied, feeling firmly put in his place.

"If you'll excuse me, I'll finish dressing for dinner. Then you can have the bathroom."

Head high, she padded to the closet, pulled a frothy yellow dress off a hanger and disappeared into the other room.

Cari soon discovered that she'd underestimated the difficulty of their absurd situation by exponential degrees.

Decently clothed in her faithful scoop-necked tea-length cocktail dress in bright canary-yellow chiffon, her hair swept up and her makeup in place, she tried to ignore the sounds emanating from the bathroom. Strange, she'd never realized before that waiting for a man while he showered could be such an intimate act.

Josh hummed a popular, bluesy tune, his rich baritone floating over the patter of the water. Cari rubbed her arm to erase the ripples of sensation his voice raised, then prickled all over again when she heard the thunk of soap dropping. Immediately the image of his hard, muscled body all sudsy and lathered sprang into her mind.

Gulping, she sank into the soft leather sofa. This was crazy. She didn't even like the man. Much. She had no business imagining him wearing nothing but soapsuds and an eye patch.

Drumming her fingers on the arm of the sofa, she tried to channel her thoughts to the sixteenth century. Unfortunately, every time she envisioned a gentleman in a white ruff, slashed doublet, tight hose and bulging codpiece, he bore an uncanny resemblance to a certain twentieth-century rogue.

Cari's cheeks warmed as a wayward thought crept into her mind. During medieval times, the codpiece had been a simple, utilitarian flap at the front of men's breeches. By the Elizabethan era, it had evolved into a separate article of clothing that males often padded for, ah, effect. From her brief contact with Josh's hard, muscular body in his hotel room, Cari suspected he wouldn't require padding. Of any sort.

Moments later, the shower shut off. She breathed a sigh of relief—prematurely, as it turned out. More water splashed into the sink, and then the scent of spicy shaving lotion drifted through the closed door.

Another image leaped into her mind. Of Josh. At the marble sink. A towel wrapped around his lean flanks. Sleek muscles rippling as he rasped a razor down his cheeks. Cari felt the glide of each slow stroke against her own skin. Her heart thumped with a loud, painful beat. Her nails dug into her palms.

Good grief, was he going to spend all night in there?

Desperate for distraction, she snatched up one of the books she'd stacked on the coffee table. She was still staring at the same page when Josh emerged from the bathroom some time later.

"Ready to go up on deck?" he asked. "Or would you like a drink first?"

Cari glanced up, a polite refusal forming. The words got stuck somewhere in the middle of her throat and stayed there.

Josh Keegan in black eye patch, tight pants and a billowing white shirt was enough to make great-grandmothers conjure up erotic fantasies. In tan slacks and red knit shirt, he'd had pretty much the same effect on Cari earlier this afternoon.

In exquisitely tailored midnight-blue slacks, a starched light blue shirt and an ivory linen jacket, he literally took her breath away. Of course, the lop-sided smile he'd wound up, and the deep mahogany tints glistening in his still-damp hair, might have something to do with her sudden breathlessness.

Oh, Lord! Cari had said she wasn't in his league. The truth was, she didn't populate the same universe as this sophisticated, self-assured, eye-watering hunk of male perfection. She managed to keep from gaping—barely—and propelled herself off the sofa.

"We might as well go upstairs and get it over with."

Chuckling, he tucked her arm in his. "Do you think you could manage a smile? Or a soulful look or two? This is supposed to be a honeymoon, not a funeral."

"Shows what you know," she muttered.

Just a few hours ago, she'd been stretched content-edly in a deck chair, contemplating ten days of bone-less, mindless relaxation. Now she was shivering with tension.

"I'm a terrible liar," she warned. "I've never been able to pull off even the littlest social lies. I hate the idea of spending the whole evening, not to mention the remainder of the cruise, pretending to the rest of the passengers that we're married."

"You're not pretending. We are."

"Temporarily."

"Temporarily."

Some vacation, she thought glumly as he led her to the door. For the next week, she'd have to watch every word she spoke, force every gesture.

Then Josh patted her hand reassuringly, and Cari's fingers curled around his arm. Under layers of linen and starched cotton, she could feel hard, smooth muscles.

Okay, so maybe she wouldn't have to force every single gesture. Still, this was not her idea of a vacation *or* a honeymoon.

Five

_____

Within five minutes of joining Captain Paxton and the other passengers under the royal-blue awning that shielded the forward half of the sun deck, Cari realized she wouldn't have to lie. She wouldn't have to say anything at all, in fact. If she wished, her part in the charade could consist of blushing, smiling and clinging to Josh's arm, all of which she could do without opening her mouth.

The groom was the undisputed star of the show. Aside from a few gushing comments to Cari about her luck in snaring such an incredible prize, the women did nothing but fawn all over him. Even silver-haired Evelyn Sanders, grandmother of Cari's surly teenage dinner partner, simpered at Josh. Clutching her predinner cocktail in fingers ringed with diamonds, she demanded the details of the whirlwind secret courtship and marriage.

"But when did you meet Cari? I could have sworn I read an article recently that said you and Jessica Hope were..." Her blue eyes widened, and she sent the bride an apologetic glance. "Oh, I'm sorry, dear. How gauche of me. Do forgive me."

Cari murmured something unintelligible and tried not to groan. Jessica Hope? Who was going to believe that mousy Caren O'Donnell, unemployed history professor, had snatched the prize of the decade away from sultry redheaded Jessica Hope, TV star?

Josh stepped smoothly into the breach. He patted Cari's hand and answered the older woman with a crooked smile that made her blink—several times.

"You shouldn't believe everything you read in the papers, Mrs. Sanders. There hasn't been any other woman in my life since I met Cari."

Cari did a quick mental calculation. She and Josh had met approximately forty-four hours ago. If there hadn't been another woman in his life since then, it just might be a new record for him.

"Please, call me Evelyn," Mrs. Sanders insisted, with a flutter of impossibly long lashes.

A younger woman in a purple silk jumpsuit and a half ton of gold jewelry picked up the refrain. "Tell us all the details, Josh! How did you two meet?"

"And when?" a third put in.

"And where?" Evelyn queried.

As she listened to the chorus of demands, Cari's first taste of sharing the spotlight with an honest-to-goodness celebrity left an odd taste in her mouth. Really, these people acted as though Josh were public property. As though he had no right to any personal thoughts or secrets. Their persistence didn't seem to faze him, though. He fielded their questions with a deftness she could only admire, and answered every query with perfect, if somewhat shaded, truth.

"We met at a party," he replied, slanting Cari an intimate, throat-closing glance. "We haven't known each other long. Just long enough to decide we wanted to get married."

Evelyn Sanders sighed. "Love at first sight. How romantic."

A noisy slurp at the older woman's side drew everyone's attention to the teenager Cari had privately dubbed Eric the Terrible. The gold ring in the boy's left nostril quivered as he took another swig of his soft drink, then gave his grandmother a pitying look.

"Get real, Gram. If it's so romantic, how come they had to sneak aboard separately? And why aren't they wearing wedding rings? I bet they're not really married, just fooling around."

Cari kept her smile pasted on her face as her nails dug into Josh's sleeve. Good grief! She hadn't thought about a ring. Nor had her groom, evidently. She waited to hear how he would tap-dance his way out of that one.

Fortunately, Paul Sanders preempted Josh's response by shooting his grandson a stern look. "Eric! Mr. Keegan explained about the need to avoid a full-court media press. Of course he couldn't wear a wedding ring in public. Let's give him a break here."

A beefy, balding man who'd made a fortune in the cement business, Sanders still carried himself with a rugged air of authority that silenced his grandson.

"Besides," Sanders, Sr., added, his gray eyes twinkling, "I want to hear what Josh thinks of Trevino's chances of winning the Senior PGA championship. Lee's my man," he confided to the assembled group.

"I played a round with him once in a pro-am at Pebble Beach. I used to swing a mean club myself, before arthritis got to me."

To Cari's intense relief, the conversation shifted from romance to golf. The other men all joined in, as did the women. Their knowledge of the game didn't surprise Cari. Every passenger aboard the *Nautilus III* except her was a member of the country club set.

She listened with interest to a lively conversation sprinkled with terminology that was unfamiliar and at times incomprehensible to her. No dummy, she soon grasped that crunching the ball was good, and shanking it wasn't. She also learned that a drive to the green didn't necessarily involve a motorized golf cart. But the arm Josh hooked around her waist with seeming casualness destroyed any hope of sorting out the difference between lateral and standing water hazards.

He was only playing his bridegroom role, Cari reminded herself. He'd rested that hand just above the curve of her hip solely for effect. Unfortunately, its effect on Cari blurred even more the confused lines between reality and make-believe.

In her wildest dreams, she had never imagined herself standing on the upper deck of a sleek white yacht, her chiffon skirts fluttering in a balmy tropical breeze, while the nineties' answer to Errol Flynn held her nestled against his side. Every time Josh sent her one of those looks that were somehow public and very, very private at the same time, their fuzzy relationship seemed to haze a bit more around the edges.

By the time he'd seated her at a candlelit table laden with crystal and silver, Cari was hovering on the dangerous edge of forgetting that she was only a pretend bride. Her groom was so attentive, so considerate, so blasted sexy.

She dragged in a deep breath and tried to hang on to reality with both hands. Resolutely she ignored the twinkle of lights against the deepening purple of Nassau's harbor. Firmly, she refused to be seduced by her first melting taste of squab à l'orange stuffed with herbed rice. Deliberately, she tuned out the sensual cadence of Josh's deep voice.

She'd walked away from one near disaster with a man who was all wrong for her. She'd darn well better keep her wits about her until she'd walked away from this one. In seven days, she reminded herself sternly, she'd be a divorced woman. In ten, she'd be back in her cluttered, comfortable apartment, buried in research books and facing down a looming deadline. Or she'd be slinging chicken and biscuits during the day while she circulated résumés and tried to salvage what she could of her years of work.

That sobering thought got Cari through dinner with both feet planted firmly on the teakwood deck. Unreality tugged at her again, however, when the chef rolled out a three-tiered wedding cake and champagne corks started popping.

Captain Paxton stood, a wide smile on his weathered, whiskered face. "On behalf of the passengers and crew, I'd like to offer a toast to the bride and groom. May your days be filled with sunswept fairways, your nights with long, straight irons, and the years ahead with a whole league of junior golfers."

"Hear! Hear!" Paul Sanders echoed, holding up his glass.

Through the spate of laughter and good wishes that followed, Cari wished fervently that she could sink under the table. She felt like an impostor. Worse than an impostor. A complete and utter fraud.

Josh slipped a hand under her arm, dragging her up with him as he rose. With unruffled charm, he acknowledged the toast and the passengers' wishes for a happy future, then picked up a champagne flute. The gold flecks in his hazel eye gleamed as he surveyed her hot face.

"To my blushing bride."

He took a long swallow, then held the tall goblet to Cari's lips. She had the choice of downing the fizzy wine or wearing it. Flashing him a grim warning not to carry this charade too far, she sipped the champagne.

Josh wasn't quite sure what made him want to take Cari up on that unspoken challenge. It might be the stern message in her brown eyes. Or the prim way she pursed her lips as she sipped. Or his ingrained habit of grandstanding for the crowd after a tricky shot. Whatever it was, he felt the damnedest urge to replace the cool crystal with his mouth. Hard on the heels of that came the instant and irrational urge to take her back below decks, pull the pins from her upswept hair and tumble her into that fairway-size bed. Which was exactly what he might have done if he hadn't been married to her. With some effort, Josh forced his thoughts away from the erotic image of Cari's creamy skin displayed against a background of pale satin.

Smart, Keegan! Real smart! Confuse the situation even more by seducing the woman you intend to divorce in a few days.

"Now cut the cake," Evelyn Sanders urged gaily.

He'd better keep a tight rein on himself and his wayward thoughts, Josh decided as he escorted his bride to the wheeled cart. And he'd darn well better curb his natural inclination to joke and tease and play to the gallery. Cari had told him bluntly that she wasn't up to his kind of game. In spite of the fact that Josh didn't know how to play it any other way, he had enough on his mind right now without the complication of a casual affair.

As Cari took the long knife the steward handed her, Josh found himself pondering the question of whether a man could have an affair, casual or otherwise, with his wife.

The flicker of dismay that crossed her face when she surveyed the cake dragged his attention back from the philosophical aspects of their marriage to the immediate realities. She wasn't enjoying this farce, he realized. At all. The hand holding the knife was wavering, and her smile was growing more ragged by the second.

"Here, let me help you."

Josh reached around her and closed his big hand over hers. It trembled in his hold, like a small, captured bird. Together, they raised the knife over the two-tiered cake.

"Wait!" Paul Sanders interjected. "You need a picture of this for your wedding album. Eric, run to our cabin and get the camera."

The teenager gave his grandfather a disgusted look.

"Now, son. Move."

Eric scraped his chair back and ambled toward the stairs.

"Hold the pose for a moment," the senior Sanders requested. "In the meantime, we'll refill the champagne glasses."

Under the clink of glass on glass and convivial conversation, Josh leaned down to put his lips close to Cari's ear.

"You okay?"

"No," she replied in a low, dejected voice. "This a spice cake. Can you believe it? A spice cake."

He believed it. The tangy scent of cinnamon and nutmeg provided ample evidence of the fact.

"Don't you like spice cake?"

"Yes," she mumbled, blinking furiously. "I do. Especially the kind my neighbor, Mrs. Wilder, bakes."

Josh was still trying to figure that one out when Eric sauntered back, carelessly dangling an expensive camera by its strap.

"Okay, now put both arms around her and get ready to cut the cake," Sanders, Sr., commanded, squinting through the viewfinder. "Good. Good. Hold it a few seconds while I adjust the shutter speed."

A few seconds stretched into long minutes as the amateur photography enthusiast fiddled with lenses and settings and camera angles. Through it all, Josh kept Cari in a loose embrace, breathing in an enticing combination of lemon-scented shampoo and spicy cinnamon.

The top of her head just brushed the underside of his chin. He refused to think about the way her firm, rounded tush brushed parts lower than his chin. Still, a slow, familiar tightening began to coil low in his body as the feel of her small, delicious body imprinted itself on his senses. To his disgust, he was wire-tight by the time Evelyn Sanders called out in exasperation.

"For heavens sake, Paul! Take the picture, already."

"All right, all right." The would-be photographer made another minute adjustment, then retreated behind the viewfinder once again. "Smile, you two. This will be one to show your grandkids."

By the time they'd cut the cake and rejoined the others at the table, Josh's smile was getting as ragged around the edges as Cari's. Fortunately, they had an out. A built-in excuse to go below early. As Evelyn Sanders said with a titter when Josh slid back his chair some time later and made their good-nights, they *were* on their honeymoon, after all.

Cari's face burned when they left to the accompaniment of envious smiles from the women and sly grins from the men. As soon as the cabin door shut behind them, she tossed her beaded bag on the sofa and spun around to face Josh.

"That was awful!"

He was inclined to agree. His body's response every time he got within touching distance of this woman disturbed the hell out of him. The stinging accusation in her brown eyes right now didn't particularly ease his discomfort, either. She acted as though this whole mess were his fault.

"I feel like such a fraud!"

"Well, you shouldn't," he replied shortly.

Too shortly, it appeared. Her chin tilted at an angle he was beginning to recognize.

"Please *do not* remind me again we're married! You know as well I do that silly ceremony we went through doesn't mean we're really..." She waved a hand helplessly.

"Married?" Josh supplied with a nasty smile, shrugging out of his linen sport coat. He tossed it over the back of the sofa and yanked at his tie. "I'm afraid it does, sweetheart."

"Not in any way that matters," she retorted. "Not in the happily-ever-after, till-death-do-us-part way."

Josh tossed his tie on top of the jacket. "Do you really believe there is a happily-ever-after? Outside of fairy tales?"

"I used to," she replied, hugging her arms. "I'm not so sure anymore."

Josh cocked his head, watching as shadows chased across her face. His brief spurt of irritability faded, replaced by a sudden curiosity about this woman who got teary-eyed over spice cake, owned more plants than furniture and was reputed to be brilliant but unreliable. Shoving his hands into his pants pockets, he leaned his hips against the back of the sofa.

"I take it you owe your growing disillusionment to more than just our imminent divorce. Want to tell me about him?"

She drew a slow pattern in the carpet with the tip of one shoe. "Not particularly."

Josh wanted to probe further, but the closed look on her face told him that subject was out of bounds.

"Then why don't you tell me how you lost your job at Billings, and why this grant is so important to you?"

Her head jerked up. "Who told you I lost it?"

Surprised at her indignation, Josh searched his memory. "You did. Or maybe Grant did."

Her feathery brows snapped together. "Grant? As in Dr. Grant?"

The sharpness in her voice told Josh he'd hit a nerve. "The same."

"You talked to Edward?"

Edward, was it? Josh guessed he'd just discovered the reason for her disillusionment. He hadn't thought much of the pompous professor, either.

"I did."

Cari planted her hands on her hips. "He told you I'd been fired?"

"He may not have said that, exactly, but he implied it."

"That...that puling caitiff!"

"Right," Josh drawled. "Exactly the way I would have described him."

She glared at him a moment longer, and then a reluctant smile pulled at her lips. "*Caitiff* is an archaic term, meaning, ah, *scoundrel.*"

"Scoundrel?" He arched one brow. "Why do I suspect you're not giving me the exact twentieth-century translation?"

"Because I don't use those kinds of four-letter words," she replied prissily. Then her brown eyes gleamed with a vibrant laughter that zinged through Josh like a runaway laser. "I think them, though."

Lord, she was tempting. A half-size bundle of generous curves covered in layers of sunshine yellow, with eyes that held more sparkle than the sea just off the fifth hole at Maui's spectacular Kapalua Bay resort.

Josh knew darn well he'd better pull back. Terminate this conversation before his casual interest in Cari O'Donnell...Cari O'Donnell Keegan...crossed the invisible boundary between curiosity and fascination.

Instead, he found himself pulling a hand from his pocket and gesturing toward the L-shaped leather sofa.

"Since we don't have any more pressing plans for the evening, why don't you get comfortable and tell me more about ol' Edward?"

She hesitated, then sank down onto the air-soft leather. Following his example, she kicked off her shoes, crossed her ankles and rested her stockinged feet on the sturdy oak-and-brass coffee table. She had small feet, he noted. Small and delicately shaped, like the rest of her. When she wiggled her toes under their nylon covering, Josh suddenly understood why men's locker rooms often sported an array of magazines that touted such things as foot fetishes—among other things. There was something damn sexy about a woman's foot. About Cari's foot, anyway.

"What else did Edward say about me?" she asked.

Josh ended his contemplation of her curling, wiggling toes. "Not much. Only that you left Billings abruptly, under questionable circumstances."

"They weren't questionable. Not to me, anyway."

Josh sensed that talking about what had happened wasn't easy for her. All too used to hiding his own thoughts and feelings behind a public facade, he didn't push her.

"Our fields closely overlapped," she said at last, leaning her head against the sofa's high back. "That was what drew me to Billings in the first place. I was thrilled at the chance to work with a recognized expert in Tudor political history. Edward's treatise on the influence of the weavers' guild during the reign of Henry VII is a textbook for any student of that period."

"I'll take your word for that," Josh put in laconically.

"His recent paper on Tudor efforts to strengthen the English wool trade contributed even more depth and insight into the era."

Josh tried to look suitably impressed.

"It also," she added with a tight smile, "incorporated a great deal of my research."

"He plagiarized your work?"

"Actually, he claimed I'd plagiarized his. That's when I tossed his ring and my position at his head and walked out."

His ring. That explained a lot, particularly her comments about not wanting to be married to anyone, not in this century.

"Why didn't you challenge him?" Josh asked. "There must be some kind of faculty board you could take your complaint to."

"There is, but in this instance, it would come down to a case of my word against his. Since I'm a . . . since I *was* a lowly assistant professor at the time, and he's chairman of the department, we both knew whose reputation would carry the most weight."

A competitor to the bone, Josh had never picked up his ball and walked off the course in his life. "So you just gave up?"

"No, I didn't just give up," Cari replied, lifting her head to shoot him a haughty look. "I put five years of hard work into my doctoral program. I'll have to modify my thesis to avoid the areas Edward covered in his paper, but I refuse to drop out of the program now, when I'm so close to completion."

Then she spoiled her effect by wrinkling her nose and descending from haughty to very human. "Besides, I wouldn't give Edward the satisfaction."

"Good for you."

"That's why I need this grant," she confided. "It will give me enough to live on while I rework the thrust of my thesis."

"And if you don't get the grant?"

She tried for nonchalance, but Josh caught the banked determination in her brown eyes. "Then I'll fall back and regroup. One way or another, I'll finish my doctorate. It may take another five years, but I'll finish."

"Why is it so important to you?"

The question seemed to surprise her. She sat up, curling her stockinged feet under her. "A doctorate is a necessary requirement for advancement in my profession. Like, what—hitting a hole-in-one in yours?"

Josh started to tell her that it took a whole lot more than a single lucky shot to qualify for the PGA tour, but her next comment pulled him up short.

"I don't want to be stuck as a lowly assistant professor all my life, any more than you want to be stuck where you are now."

"Just where do you think I am now?"

She blinked at the sudden chill in his voice. "I don't know. From the way everyone fawns all over you, I suppose you're at or near the top of your career. But you're what—thirty-seven? Thirty-eight?"

"Thirty-four."

"Really? It must be the patch," she tacked on hastily, when she saw his scowl. "But that just proves my point. At thirty-four, you must have goals you still want to achieve."

He had goals, all right, but Josh didn't know whether he'd ever achieve them. He wouldn't know, until he got back to Atlanta and started swinging a club again. He wasn't quite ready to talk about them, however. Not even to Cari of the sexy toes.

Rising, he stretched and gave her his best Josh Keegan grin. "Right now, my only goal is to talk you into sharing that bed. Sure you won't reconsider? I've been told I don't snore, and I promise I won't hog the covers."

As he'd expected, a wash of pink collared her throat and warmed her cheeks. But instead of rising to his bait, she tilted her head and gave him a steady look.

"You're good at that, aren't you?"

"What? Not hogging the covers?"

"No, turning aside personal questions with a grin and a joke. I watched you do it with the other passengers tonight, and now you're doing it with me."

He waggled his brows. "What makes you think I'm joking, little girl?"

"You're doing it again."

The quiet observation pierced the protective armor Josh pulled on like a second skin whenever anyone got too close. This time, he made an effort to give her an honest answer.

"It's a survival skill I learned early in my career. I kid around a lot and tell the media only what I want them to hear. I also try to listen selectively to what they say about me."

"Sounds like that might be easier said than done."

"You got that right."

Josh rubbed the back of his neck, remembering some of his less-than-successful encounters with the media. One in particular remained emblazoned on his memory. To his surprise, he found himself telling Cari about it.

"During my first U.S. Open, one of the announcers made a casual remark about my swing. If I'd been smarter, or older, or more seasoned, I might not have paid any attention to it. But I wasn't. For the rest of the tournament, I tried to correct a problem that didn't really exist. In the process, I managed to take myself from third place after the first round to dead last."

"Oh, no!"

"Golf is one percent skill and ninety-nine percent concentration," he replied with a shrug. "It's easy to lose that concentration. Since that incident, I've learned to filter what's said or written about me and my game."

He'd also learned that sports announcers were pussycats compared to tabloid reporters. *They* ate unsuspecting prey alive.

They'd devour Cari whole, he thought. She'd barely made it through dinner with a few inquisitive passengers. If a pack of headline-hungry reporters descended on her, she'd come apart at the seams. Guilt rippled through him at the realization of what he'd gotten her into, along with a determination to shield her as much as possible from the less pleasant aspects of association with a celebrity.

"The pressure of living in the spotlight can be relentless, Cari. With a little luck and a fast, quiet divorce, we might get you through this mess relatively unscarred."

"Relatively?"

"By the time we get back from Cancún and the story leaks, as it undoubtedly will, our marriage will be history."

Josh wondered why the hell the idea didn't give him the satisfaction it should.

"I'll come up with something equally newsworthy to make our supposed romance old news," he promised.

Like announcing his return to the tour. Or his retirement. Josh shoved aside that last grim possibility.

"Now, about the bed..."

Battling wildly conflicting emotions, Cari hesitated. A part of her hated for these quiet moments to end. The brief glimpse Josh had given her of the man behind the cocky media idol intrigued her. He was human enough to be thrown off stride by an offhand remark. And intelligent enough to learn from that experience. She wanted to discover more about this Josh Keegan.

Another part of her, a very female part, responded involuntarily to the teasing glint in his hazel eye. For a wild, sizzling moment, she imagined what it would be like to accede to his request. To invite him to share the huge bed. To tuck herself into the curve of that lean, muscled body. To turn their pretended, enforced intimacy into an honest-to-goodness honeymoon.

The impossibility of that pulled her up short. In her heart of hearts, Cari believed a honeymoon meant more than just two bodies tangled up in the sheets. It meant love. And commitment. And, darn it, a sense of forever. All of which Josh Keegan, playboy of the western world, obviously didn't believe in.

No, her engagement to Edward had put a few serious dents in her illusions, but she wasn't ready to give

them up completely. Shaking her head, she sent Josh
a cheery smile.

"No way, Keegan. You get the couch. But I will give
you first dibs on the bathroom."

Six

Josh had expected that sharing a cabin with Cari might lead to an awkward moment or two. He hadn't expected to spend the entire first night of his so-called honeymoon wide awake and staring at the ceiling while his wife tossed and turned with maddening frequency.

She wasn't a quiet sleeper. Every time she flopped over, her arm hit the mattress with a *whump*. Whenever her legs scissored on the satiny sheets, the sound hissed in his ears. Occasionally, she huffed. There was no other word for it. She pushed out little, breathy puffs of air that carried clearly to the sofa across the cabin. Once, she sat straight up and mumbled something about pieces of cod, of all things, then toppled down onto the pillows and yanked the covers over her head. At that point, Josh considered his choices.

His first was to tie her to the bed. Somehow he suspected she might not appreciate that solution.

His second was to climb under the covers and anchor her restless body so tightly against his that she wouldn't be able to thump her arms or legs or anything else. She'd probably appreciate that solution even less.

His third also involved climbing into bed. Only this option included a few extras. Like playing footsie with her sexy little toes. And burying his face in that silky-soft banana-colored hair. And making wild, extravagant love to her, over and over, until she was so exhausted and limp from pleasure that she couldn't move, much less flop and thump against the mattress.

Unfortunately, the more Josh thought about the last option, the less he could sleep. He lay wide awake, listening to the sounds from the other end of the suite until he was rock-hard and aching. If this hadn't been the first night of his blasted honeymoon, he might have gone on deck to cool down. Or to the exercise room to sweat the wire-tight tension out of his muscles and the image of Cari all sleepy and languid from lovemaking out of his mind. Since he was supposed to be wrapped in his bride's arms, however, all he could do was give his own pillow a solid whack or two, turn over, and try to sleep.

The sound of another *whump* jerked him awake some hours later. He sat up, relieved to see a hazy blue-gray light sneaking under the drawn curtains. Tossing aside the spare blanket Cari had found in a closet, he rose and stretched. In T-shirt and briefs, he padded to the closet and slid its mirrored panel sideways on its silent, well-oiled rollers.

Not wanting to wake Cari by turning on a light, he groped around until he found his gray jersey sweats and tennis shoes. Once dressed, he folded the blanket and stowed it away. Then he settled down on the couch again to wait for the time a new groom might reasonably be expected to go topside in search of a cup of coffee.

Cari was still sleeping when he let himself out of the cabin, some time later. She was up and dressed by the time he returned, bearing a covered tray.

Josh stopped short just over the threshold, transfixed by the sight of his bride in the soft light of morning. She had anchored her hair in a loose twist on top of her head with a plastic thingamabob, leaving only a few tendrils to brush her cheeks. The morning light gleamed on her translucent skin. In a sleeveless, vestlike top of deep indigo, white shorts and white canvas shoes, she looked cool and comfortable. And decidedly nervous, Josh noted.

"Good morning."

Her tentative, almost shy greeting would have triggered a smile in Josh, if he hadn't suddenly felt just a bit off center himself. Which was crazy. This wasn't one of those awkward morning-afters. They hadn't shared anything more intimate than the same general airspace last night. Yet he had to force his voice to its usual lazy drawl as he strolled into the cabin with his laden tray.

"Mornin'. I brought us some coffee and rolls and fruit. But there's a full buffet upstairs, if you're a big breakfast eater."

She hesitated. "Is everyone already topside?"

"Most of them."

Hunching her shoulders, she tucked her hands into her pockets. As she did, the midnight-blue vest lifted and bared a strip of pale, concave midriff. Josh's fingers tightened around the tray. He could now add an intriguing belly button to the inventory of sparkling eyes, creamy skin and sexy toes.

"Why don't we just eat here?" she suggested. "Or on our deck?"

Josh hefted the tray on one palm, waiter-style. "Lead the way, madame."

With a wider, more relaxed smile, she crossed the suite and pulled open the drapes on the sliding glass doors. Dazzling sunlight spilled into the cabin, turning the pale carpet to a sea of liquid gold. Outside, a royal-blue awning shaded half of a private deck just large enough for a round table and four swivel chairs, all of which were bolted down. Beyond the deck rail, an aquamarine bay dotted with bobbing white sailboats stretched across the horizon.

Josh felt a leap of pleasure that he didn't stop to define at the thought of sharing a quiet breakfast and this spectacular view with Cari. He waved her to a chair, then proceeded to serve her with all the pomp and dignity of a world-class maître d'.

"So, madame." He whipped off the napkins covering the baskets on the tray. "We have here ze muffins. We have ze croissants with strawberry jam. And ze papaya and ze mango and..." He broke off, frowning at several brown, hairy balls. "What are these, anyway? Baby coconuts?"

"They're kiwi," she replied, smiling.

He poked an exploratory finger at the fruit. "I thought kiwi was green."

"It is," she told him, her smile slipping into a grin. "Inside. You have to peel it."

"Tell you what—you peel and I'll pour."

"Fair enough."

Cari was amazed at how quickly Josh's light-hearted banter helped diminish the unease that had dogged her from the moment she woke up this morning.

The inquisition from the other passengers at dinner last night had been bad enough. Toasting her groom and cutting into the surprise wedding cake with their good wishes ringing in her ears had made her feel even worse. But the thought of facing Evelyn Sanders and the others in the bright light of morning, after a night of supposedly rapturous passion in Josh's arms, totally daunted her. Cari knew she couldn't pull that one off.

Not that she was inexperienced at rapture, exactly. She and Edward had explored the full scope of their relationship. But somehow Cari suspected that Josh Keegan's brand of lovemaking would leave a different physical and emotional mark on her than anything she'd ever experienced before. *Very* different.

As Josh wrestled with the top of one of those so-called easy-pour carafes, Cari studied him through the screen of her lashes. In thin gray sweats that hugged his muscular frame, he somehow managed to look even more handsome than he had in elegant evening attire. Maybe the sunlight playing on his tanned skin had something to do with it. Or the offshore breeze ruffling his dark brown hair. Or the stubble of a night's growth that shadowed his cheeks and his strong square chin.

"Got it," he exclaimed, triumph lacing his deep voice as he reached for a coffee cup.

While he poured and added creamer at her request, Cari's gaze snagged on the crease on one side of his temple caused by the strap to his eye patch. Once again she wondered about the extent of his eye injury. After the way he'd avoided answering her questions about himself last night, though, she hesitated to ask about it. For a man who lived his life in the limelight, he was a surprisingly private person.

Cari respected that privacy too much to probe. Besides, she didn't want to introduce what was undoubtedly a painful subject into this quiet, relaxing moment in the sun. Which was just as well, because the quiet came to a shattering end not two seconds later.

She'd just put a peeled and sliced kiwi on a plate when a cannonball dropped out of the sky. Or so it seemed to Cari. The huge missile came whizzing past the edge of the awning, hit the table surface with a resounding *thwack*, scattered fruit, rolls, and coffee cups, then bounced up again.

Screeching in surprise, Cari jerked backward.

Josh reached up and caught the careening object in midair. "What the hell—?"

Distracted by the white-and-black soccer ball in Josh's hands, Cari didn't notice the spilled coffee snaking across the tabletop. Searing-hot liquid splashed on her bare thigh an instant later. She gasped and swiveled her chair to one side at the same moment Eric's voice rang out.

"Hey, man, good catch!"

Unaware of Cari's efforts to dab the coffee from her stinging flesh with a napkin, Josh squinted up at the teenager hanging over the rail of the sun deck.

"Not good enough, it seems," he replied, laughing. "You just scored a goal on our breakfast."

Cari glanced up to see a huge grin splitting the boy's face.

"Eric!" Paul Sanders joined his grandson at the upper rail. "I told you not to kick that thing around the deck."

The liveliness on the boy's face drained away, and a familiar sulkiness settled over his features. "There's nothing else to do on this floating mausoleum," he protested.

"Apologize to Mr. and Mrs. Keegan," Sanders, Sr., insisted sternly.

Cari started at the form of address, then flushed a bright red. Luckily, everyone was too engaged in the small drama to notice.

"Now, Eric..."

"Sorry," the boy muttered.

"It's okay," Josh replied, sending Cari a quick look. "No real harm done, is there?"

Wadding the damp napkin in one hand, she ignored her stinging thigh. There was no point in putting the boy further in his grandfather's bad graces. He hadn't intended to bombard their breakfast table, Cari was sure. Almost sure.

"No real harm done," she agreed.

"Here you go."

Josh tossed the soccer ball up to the boy. With a smooth, fluid grace, he leaned forward to catch it, then tucked it under one arm.

"Good reflexes," Josh observed, leaning his hips against the rail to converse with the two males above him.

"Eric's on the A soccer team at school," Paul boasted, ruffling the boy's brown hair affectionately. His grandson grimaced and ducked away.

"Ever tried your hand at golf?" Josh asked the boy.

"Once or twice. With Granddad."

"Did you like it?"

Eric shrugged. "It's okay."

"Don't let him fool you, Josh. The kid's a natural. You should see his swing. It's as smooth and sweet as a baby's behind." Paul broke off, his ruddy face brightening. "Say, I brought my clubs along. Not that I've been able to use them, because of this damned arthritis. But maybe you could give Eric a few pointers sometime."

"Maybe."

Cari wasn't the only one who caught the withdrawal in Josh's voice. While she studied his face, Sanders, Sr., sputtered an apology.

"That was real bright of me, wasn't it? I forgot you're on your honeymoon. Last thing you'd want to do is give golf lessons."

Josh's eye caught Cari's. His momentary stiffness vanished, replaced by a deliberate, teasing grin. "Well, I can think of one or two other things I'd rather do," he admitted.

Paul clapped a hand on his grandson's shoulder. "C'mon, son. Let's leave these two lovebirds alone."

Cari's face flamed as she and Josh righted tumbled crockery, sopped up spilled coffee and tossed soggy rolls overboard for the fish.

"Interesting kid," Josh commented.

"Think so? He was my dinner partner before you arrived on the scene. My private name for him is Eric the Terrible."

Josh laughed as he stacked the remains of their picnic breakfast on the tray. "He's not so bad. Just bored. Hey, you didn't get anything to eat. Want to go topside and catch what's left of the buffet?"

"No, I—" She broke off, wincing, when the angry red patch on her thigh accidentally brushed the table edge.

"What's the matter?"

"It's nothing. A little spilled coffee landed in my lap, that's all."

He walked around the table. "Let me see."

"No, really. It's nothing."

His dark brows snapped together as he took in the blistered patch of skin on the inside of her thigh. "It doesn't look like nothing from this angle. Sit down. I'll check the bathroom for first aid supplies."

"I..."

"Sit down."

She didn't protest further, for the simple reason that he had already stepped through the sliding glass doors and headed for the bathroom. And if the truth were told, she'd be happy to put some ointment on the stinging burn.

Josh didn't give her the chance to doctor herself, however. Hunkering down on one knee in front of her chair, he squeezed a generous dollop of antiseptic cream onto a folded gauze pad.

"Here, this ought to do the trick. Spread your legs a bit."

Her face as hot as her seared skin, Cari eased her legs apart. Get a grip, O'Donnell, she chided herself. He was only trying to help. There was nothing the least bit sexual about the way he stroked the cream over the burn. No reason to tense as he lightly taped the gauze pad in place.

His hands were gentle, sure, steady. Hers itched to bury themselves in his crisp dark hair.

His breath warmed her already heated skin as he worked. Hers got stuck in her windpipe.

He sat back on his heel, his arm resting on his knee as he surveyed his handiwork, then glanced up at her.

"Feel better?"

Sure. Uh-huh. As if she could feel anything at all, with Josh Keegan parked so intimately between her legs.

"Yes, thank you," she managed to squeak out.

When he rose and moved back, Cari felt a surge of relief. And the strangest ripple of disappointment. Okay, more than a ripple. A medium-size wave.

"I'd better go change," she murmured, swiveling the chair away. The movement brought her thighs into contact with each other, and she couldn't help but wince again.

"Looks like you won't be strolling through Nassau's shops this morning," Josh observed.

"Or anywhere else." She sighed, glancing at the colorful palette of pastel-hued buildings lining the bay. "I'm glad I got to explore the island yesterday, since we're leaving at noon. I'll just laze in the sun today, and venture ashore when we dock at Saint Thomas tomorrow."

"Are you sure? We could take a taxi to Paradise Island Casino and try our hand at the tables. You wouldn't have to walk more than a few steps."

"The last place I want to visit on this trip is a casino," she replied with a grin. "Aside from the fact that I don't have what you'd call a poker face, I have to watch my pennies until I hear about the grant. I only came on this cruise because the prize package covered all expenses."

"I'll stake you," he offered, his gaze holding hers.

"No, thanks. But you ought to go. Even a new groom has to, ah . . ."

"Come up for air sometime?"

Her cheeks warmed, but Cari pressed her point. "Seriously, Josh, I don't think we should let this silly marriage business spoil the cruise for either one of us. You go to the casino if you want. I'll be perfectly content with my book and a deck chair in the sun."

Josh wasn't sure which sat worse with him. The idea that marriage to him was spoiling her vacation, or the thought that she'd prefer a book to his company. He wasn't any more vain than the next man. Or any more stupid. He knew darn well that most of the women who'd made themselves so available during his years on the tour had been drawn more by his media image than by any interest in the man behind the image. Still, Cari's casual dismissal put a definite dent in his ego.

"Tell you what," he suggested coolly. "I'll go up and get you some more breakfast. While you eat, we'll negotiate our agenda for the rest of the morning."

* * *

Their negotiations resulted in a compromise. Sensing that Cari was more disappointed than she would admit at missing out on her last few hours on the colorful, bustling Caribbean island, Josh suggested that he rent a car and take her on a driving tour. Her delighted smile and her eagerness for the expedition went a long way toward smoothing over the ding in his ego.

He left her for a few moments to make the necessary arrangements. When he returned, her glowing beauty made him question his judgment. Could he really spend the entire day and the coming night in the company of this vibrant woman without doing something really stupid, like implementing option three?

She'd exchanged her coffee-stained white shorts for a loose skirt in a pale yellow material sprigged with flowers in the same deep indigo as her sleeveless vest. Her hair was tucked under a hat of similar blue, its narrow brim turned up in front and pinned with a huge, artificial sunflower. She clutched an overflowing straw tote in one hand and a heavy leather-bound book in the other.

Josh relieved her of both burdens. "Can you walk, or should I carry you?"

"I can walk. Sort of." She scrunched her nose. "But you go first. I suspect my bowlegged waddle will not be a pretty sight from behind."

Grinning, he led the way down the narrow walkway outside their cabin to the hatch amidships. A burly uniformed crewman waited at the gate to the outboard stairs. Enrique. Josh decided he didn't particularly like the man. Or the way the steward's gaze slid past Josh and lingered on Cari.

"I brought the launch around for you." Unhooking the gate in the rail, Enrique swung it open. "These stairs are tricky, yes? Give me your hand, and I will guide you down."

Josh watched through narrowed eyes as Enrique's big paw closed around Cari's hand. The crewman guided her down the narrow steps with a great deal more solicitousness than Josh thought was warranted.

For the second time in the space of an hour, an unfamiliar emotion whipped through him. He'd worked his way past Cari's blithe willingness to forgo his company earlier, but he suspected he'd have to put some effort into shaking this sudden, fierce sense of possessiveness.

The sight of another man touching Cari disturbed him. Disturbed him, hell. It raised primitive male hackles he'd never known he possessed. Jaw tight, Josh hefted Cari's straw tote and moved toward the stairs.

"Where are you guys going?"

He turned to find Eric leaning against the bulkhead, both hands shoved in the pockets of his designer shorts.

"For a drive around the island."

"Oh, yeah?"

Josh hesitated, his desire to get away for a while warring with the obvious boredom on the boy's face. "What are you and your grandparents doing?"

"Gram wants to go shopping. She says Granddad and I have to go, too."

"A drag, huh?"

"You got that right."

Still Josh hesitated. The kid wasn't his problem. He and Cari were supposed to be on their honeymoon. They couldn't be expected to baby-sit a bored, nose-ringed teen. But Josh remembered his own restless energy at Eric's age, and knew how much he would have hated being cooped up on a ship full of adults.

"Would you like to come with us?"

From the downward curl of Eric's lip, Josh was sure he would refuse. Relieved, he half turned, intending to get away before the kid changed his mind.

"Yeah, I guess so."

"Oh. Okay. Go clear it with your grandparents. We'll wait for you here."

Cari took the teen's inclusion on the expedition with cheerful goodwill. She never mentioned the burn caused by the dive-bomber soccer ball, which led Josh to eye her with a good deal of respect.

Handed the map and the responsibility for navigation, Eric's prickliness gradually disappeared. He got them lost several times as they drove through the city, but each twist and turn revealed some new treasure that delighted Cari so much that no one minded the circuitous route.

"Oh, look!" she exclaimed as Josh backed up after yet another wrong turn. "There's the statue of Captain Woodes Rogers."

"Weird-looking guy," Eric muttered, peering at the stone figure standing guard outside the pink-and-white British Colonial Hotel.

"Rogers was a South Sea privateer, so scarred from battle that he had only half a face," Cari explained.

"The British king appointed him to subdue the pirates who ruled the Bahamas and restore order."

"Real pirates? No kidding. Hey, did any of them wear patches, like Josh?"

Josh's hand tightened on the steering wheel as he remembered his costume the night he'd met Cari—and his offers to play pirate with her. Since last night, the fantasy had gained a real hold in his mind.

"Eye injuries from sword slashes or pistol burns were common in those times," she answered Eric. "A number of men wore patches."

"Cool."

Encouraged by the teen's interest, she expanded on the topic a bit. "Actually, Nassau used to be known as Charles Town, until the Spanish sacked and burned it in a futile effort to drive out the likes of Blackbeard, Henry Morgan and Anne Boney. The town was rebuilt a year later, and rechristened Nassau in honor of the new king, William III, of Orange-Nassau."

Eric draped his long, gangly arms over the front seat. "How do you know so much about these guys?"

"It's my job. I teach history."

"Yuck."

"You didn't think history was so yucky a moment ago," she replied, laughing.

"Okay, maybe this stuff isn't so bad. Tell me more about the pirates. Like, did they really force prisoners to sign papers with their own blood? And make them walk the plank? And fly the skull and crossbones on their ships?"

"Yes. No. Yes."

Leaning an elbow on the opened window, Josh steered along the narrow island roads with one hand

and listened to Eric's peppered questions and Cari's laughing responses. To his considerable surprise, he found himself as intrigued as the boy with Cari's lively interpretation of historical events.

He'd been an average student all through high school and college, more interested in sports than academics. Maybe if he'd had a teacher like Cari to snag his interest, he might have achieved something better than his solid, if not spectacular, grade point average.

He slanted her a quick glance.

Who was he kidding? If he'd had a teacher like Cari in high school or college, his hormones would have gone into instant overload and drowned out every word she said. They were pretty close to that now.

He shot her another quick look, wondering how the hell he was going to get through five more nights without touching her.

Hard on the heels of that came another, far more disturbing, thought. How the hell was he going to walk away from her five days from now?

Seven

Thirty-six hours later, Josh was still pondering the implications of his growing fascination with Cari. By this point, the problem had taken on a driving urgency.

Wrapping his palms around the teak rail, he stared out at a midnight sea. The boat rocked gently beneath him, showing only mooring lights, in deference to the late hour. Josh caught a flash of phosphorescence in the distance as a wave curled beyond the entrance to Charlotte Amalie's harbor. But the quiet beauty of the tropical night did nothing to lessen the tension that had him strung tighter than the anchor line.

He wanted to make love to his wife.

Badly.

So badly he couldn't spend another moment in their

cabin, listening to her thump the mattress and mumble in her sleep.

Yesterday had been sheer hell. Their long drive yesterday morning had been followed by a lazy afternoon aboard ship and a convivial dinner under a canopy of stars. Once Cari got past her shyness and her guilt over deceiving the others, she'd emerged as a bright, articulate dinner partner. One, Josh discovered, who remained completely unaware of her fresh, natural beauty.

Her store of historical trivia had fascinated the other passengers as much as it did Eric and Josh. At the teenager's urging, she'd entertained them all with lively stories about the rogues who'd sailed these waters. She hadn't glamorized the buccaneers, but she had balanced their daring and often brutal cruelties against the times, which could have compelled any man to desperate acts. Throughout the impromptu history lesson, she'd been in her element, dreamy and lost in another world at some moments, vibrant with laughter at others.

Josh had ached to take her in his arms when he closed the cabin door behind them after dinner. He'd barely understood his vague, primal need to anchor her in his world, not the swashbuckling era she seemed to prefer. Then he'd lain awake most of the night listening to her mumbly, twitching sleep sounds and devising ever more erotic ways to stifle them.

As bad as yesterday had been, however, today had been worse. Much worse.

With its sophisticated satellite navigation and communications systems, the *Nautilus III* had made the long sea leg between Nassau and Saint Thomas in the

U.S. Virgin Islands in good time. Early this morning, they'd dropped anchor in the harbor of Charlotte Amalie, which nestled like a pink-and-white birthday cake against the island's steep green hills. At that point, Josh had made a serious strategic error.

In the face of Cari's stubborn refusal to let him stake her to a visit to shops filled with every imaginable luxury, he'd suggested a picnic on one of the narrow, pristine white beaches hugging the shoreline. When she convinced him that salt water would aid the healing process of her burn, their picnic had become a snorkeling excursion. Somehow, Eric had ended up joining them...which was all that had saved Cari from being tumbled onto the sand and made hard, hot, furious love to.

Josh dug his nails into the wooden rail as he remembered the sight of her curvaceous legs slicing the green waters just a few feet from his face mask. He was sure he'd see those legs and that firm, rounded bottom in his dreams for the next couple of decades. Watching her delighted exploration of the treasures of the sea, Josh had gone hard with need, so hard he was surprised he hadn't sunk like a stone to the bottom of the bay. That was the longest, most uncomfortable swim he'd ever endured.

Back aboard the *Nautilus III*, Cari and Eric had chattered on and on about the fantastically colored coral and fish they'd seen. All the while, Josh had fought the almost overpowering urge to haul her back to their cabin, peel off that old-fashioned bathing suit and ravish her as he had jokingly offered to do.

It wasn't a joke anymore.

Not that he'd have to resort to silken bonds or teasing torture. Despite the fact that Cari hadn't given him the least encouragement, she couldn't disguise her increasing awareness of him, any more than he could hide his desire for her.

The only thing that kept Josh from climbing in beside her in that endless bed was what would happen when they climbed out of it. Sometime in the past few days, Josh had come to the painful realization he wasn't interested in a casual, short-lived affair with Cari.

He wanted…more. What, he wasn't quite sure, but he knew it involved more than a roll in champagne-colored sheets.

Unfortunately, he was fresh out of "mores" to offer her. He had no business speculating about a future that included Cari, when his future was so uncertain. Until he returned to Atlanta and proved just what he could or couldn't do with this damn patch over his eye, he had no right to disrupt her life…any more than he already had.

Frustration ate at him like old, corrosive acid. Turning away from the beauty of the moonlit sea, he paced the narrow walkway leading from the darkened sun deck to the forward part of the ship. His rubber-soled deck shoes squeaked on the varnished wood, but the faint sound was lost in the lapping of the waves against the hull. As Josh neared the bridge, he caught the greenish glow from navigational instruments and the silhouette of the white-uniformed captain at the communications panel.

"Right, we'll be there tomorrow night, as scheduled."

Tomorrow night? By "there," Josh supposed the captain meant Saint John, the smallest of the U.S. Virgin Islands. They were scheduled to drop anchor and attend some kind of pig roast or something. The day after the pig roast, Josh remembered suddenly, the *Nautilus III* would cruise to Grand Cayman, the last stop on their itinerary before Cancún.

Josh's stomach clenched so tightly he missed the captain's next words. He couldn't, however, miss the angry curse that followed a few seconds later.

"Dammit, you don't have to worry about Keegan being aboard. I told you, no one else knows. Don't get snakebit on me, Salazar. Just make our rendezvous as scheduled."

A moment later, Captain Paxton signed off and tossed the hand-held radio transmitter onto the console. Muttering another curse, he wiped a hand over a beard streaked to a whiskey brown by the sun. His hand jerked when he saw Josh step into the command center of the boat.

"Got a problem, Captain?"

Paxton's eyes narrowed on Josh's face for long moments, as if he were trying to gauge how much he'd heard.

"Not one I can't handle," he replied at last.

"But one that involves me."

Paxton let his breath out on a gusty sigh. "I guess you heard from my conversation that one of my suppliers knows you're aboard. 'Fraid that was my fault. He and I go way back, and I let something slip a few days ago."

A few days ago?

Surprise replaced Josh's swift, instinctive tension. In those few days, Paxton's contact could have sold the story to the tabloids and called in a full brigade of media, but he'd chosen not to. For some reason. Josh should have felt nothing but relief over the reprieve. Instead, the suspicion that he was being set up snaked through him. He pinned the captain with a level stare.

"I got the impression that my presence aboard the *Nautilus III* makes your friend nervous."

"It does," Paxton admitted, a grin creasing his weathered skin. "Very nervous."

"Want to tell me why?"

"This particular supplier ran into some trouble with the U.S. Navy a few years ago. A little misunderstanding about the grade of diesel fuel he was selling them. Since then, he's maintained, shall we say, a low profile in his business dealings."

In other words, Josh guessed, the guy was bootlegging fuel that didn't meet the strict environmental standards the U.S. imposed on its suppliers. And Paxton was buying it.

Josh had heard that a good number of shipowners in the U.S. were under investigation for the same practice. The fact that this was a ship cruising international waters fuzzed the matter considerably in his mind.

But he now understood why the captain was as anxious as Josh himself to avoid a media invasion of his ship. He was also beginning to understand how Paxton could offer a luxury cruise like this at such unbelievably low prices. If the captain was using questionable suppliers for fuel, he was probably skirting the law in other areas, as well. Josh was willing to bet the hulking Enrique didn't carry a green card.

"What are you doing up so late, Keegan?"

The casual question diverted Josh's thoughts from diesel fuel and work permits. Hooking his thumbs in the pockets of his shorts, he tried to come up with an answer that would make sense, coming from a honeymooner.

"I'm hungry."

The captain's whiskers twitched. "Worked up an appetite, huh? Now, why doesn't that surprise me? Why don't we go raid the galley? I could use a little late-night snack myself."

"Sure you don't want to go ashore with us, dear?" Evelyn Sanders asked in a heavy whisper.

Cari squinted up at the older woman. She declined the invitation with a smile, keeping her voice low, so that it wouldn't disturb the man slumbering in the deck chair beside her, a panama hat pulled down over his face.

"No, thanks."

"I found the most wonderful boutique in Charlotte Amalie yesterday that carries nothing but French imports."

"I'm not much of a shopper," Cari replied softly, sticking a finger in her book to hold its place.

One of the women clustered behind Evelyn smothered a laugh. "If I was honeymooning with Josh Keegan, I wouldn't be wasting my time in French boutiques, either. Let's go, Evelyn. Can't you see they want to be alone?"

With a final round of whispered farewells, the group of well-dressed women made their way to the outboard stairs, where Enrique and the launch waited. Cari tugged the brim of her straw hat down lower on her forehead and opened her book once more.

Despite her best efforts, she couldn't seem to concentrate. Every few paragraphs, her gaze snuck sideways. The man at her side interested her far more than the intricacies of sixteenth-century goldsmithing.

For an athlete, Josh certainly had odd sleep patterns. He didn't get much rest at night, if his increasingly haggard expression in the mornings was any indication. Each day, Cari's guilt at hogging the sublimely comfortable bed and sentencing him to the couch hitched upward another notch. As did her worry that his inability to sleep at night might have something to do with the plastic bottle of painkillers she'd glimpsed in his shaving kit. The high dosage level of the pills had shocked her. She'd had no idea he was suffering that kind of agony.

More and more, Cari longed to ask him about his injury. To recognize when he might be hurting. To cradle him in her arms and offer what comfort she could. Knowing how carefully he guarded his privacy behind that easygoing, smiling facade, she settled for making sure he got the rest he obviously needed during the day.

If and when he was ready to talk to her, he would. She hoped.

The intensity of that hope surprised her. She shouldn't harbor this longing, this fierce urge to know the real Josh Keegan. Their not-so-funny gag wedding had bound them together for this small slice of time. After the divorce, they'd probably never see each other again. It shouldn't matter to her so much that he might be hurting. But it did. Oh, Lord, it did!

"What are you guys doing?"

Closing her book once more, Cari squinted up at Eric the Not-So-Terrible.

"Soaking up some rays," she replied. "What about you? What are your plans for the day?"

Hunching his shoulders, he slumped down onto a vacant deck chair. "I don't have any. Granddad was going to charter a fishing boat today, but his arthritis is really acting up. He's resting while Gram shops."

Cari chewed on her lower lip, wondering why in the world she should feel sorry for a boy whose red polo shirt sported a designer logo recognizable the world over. She couldn't afford to buy the designer's catalogs, let alone any of his products. Still, Eric's disgruntled expression tugged at her soft heart.

"Want to play cards?"

"Yeah, I guess so."

Her eyes twinkled. "Don't overwhelm me with your enthusiasm."

Eric gave her a shamefaced grin. "Sorry. I'm just not much for sit-down games."

"What kind of games do you like—besides kamikaze soccer?"

"Basketball. Field hockey. Coach says I swing a pretty good baseball bat, too."

"Well, I can't help you out there," Cari admitted. "I was the only girl in my high school who had to take remedial gym three years in a row."

A chuckle drifted from under the panama hat. Cari glanced down as Josh lazily pushed the hat off his face.

"Three years, huh?"

"It would have been four, but poor Mrs. Lancaster fudged my grade my senior year, so she wouldn't have to face me again."

"What about college?"

Cari shuddered. "You don't want to know!"

He sat up, sharing a grin with the boy on Cari's other side. "Guess that means we won't choose her for our team in deck tennis."

Eric pretended to consider the matter. "I don't know, Josh. We might have a problem here. It's either Cari or Gram."

"Hmmm . . . I see what you mean."

Their glum faces made Cari sputter with laughter. "Hey, this particular problem suggests you two macho males go do something sweaty on your own."

"Like what?" Eric asked her challengingly, a trace of boredom creeping back into his voice.

"I don't know." She waved a hand airily. "Go swing some bats. Or some golf clubs. Didn't your grandfather say he'd brought his clubs along?"

When she saw the reaction to her careless suggestion, Cari could have bitten off her tongue. A hopeful light sprang into Eric's eyes. Josh's gaze went dead and flat. In his eagerness, the boy didn't seem to notice Josh's lack of enthusiasm.

"Hey, that would be way cool!" He hesitated, then added shyly, "Granddad thinks I've got a decent swing, but it's nothing like yours, Josh. I've seen you on TV. You're the best."

Josh glanced away from the boy, and Cari's heart lurched at the bleakness on his face. When he turned back a moment later, it was gone. The beginnings of the cocky grin he presented to the public lifted one corner of his mouth.

"Well, I've been known to hit a decent ball on occasion, but I've never tested my skills as an instructor. I'm game if you are, though."

Eric jumped up. "Really? Wow!"

Josh rose and clapped a hand over the boy's shoulder. "I'll see if the captain can rig a net on the back of the sun deck while you go get your grandfather's clubs. Then I'll watch you whack a few balls." He glanced over his shoulder. "You okay here for a while, Cari?"

She forced a smile. "I'm okay."

As she watched Josh and Eric head toward the bridge, Cari admitted to herself that she was anything but okay. Her brief glimpse of Josh's grim expression had thoroughly shaken her. Without meaning to, she'd pushed him into something he obviously didn't want to do.

She struggled to understand what that might be. Everything she'd heard, everything she'd read, about Josh suggested that golf was his passion. Golf, and a continual string of glamorous women. She'd gotten to know him well enough these past few days to understand that his playboy image was as much media hype as fact. But his reputation as a world-class golfer certainly wasn't a myth. To earn it, he'd racked up all kinds of championships.

So what had caused his lips to tighten and those deep lines to groove his cheeks a moment ago?

Maybe giving lessons was against some kind of rule for the pros. Maybe he wasn't a very good instructor, as he'd implied. Or maybe... Cari swallowed, remembering the painkillers. The accident might have destroyed his ability to concentrate. To play the game he loved.

Nervous, she watched Captain Paxton and one of the crew attach a jury-rigged aluminum frame to metal cleats on the rear railing. At Josh's suggestion, they draped two layers of fine netting over the frame and tied them in place.

"There," the captain said in satisfaction. "You couldn't whiz a mosquito through that net, much less a golf ball."

"Looks good, Captain, but we need a target. Something that will make a sound when the ball hits it."

"Hang on a second. I'll get you a nice crackly navigational map."

A few moments later, Josh tied the folded map squarely in the center of the net, then moved back to stand beside the boy. Dropping a large square of carpet down to protect the teakwood deck, he crossed his arms and grinned at the now anxious teen.

"Okay, kid, show me how you hold a club."

Eric pawed through a bag the size of a large steamer trunk. "Which club? The driver?"

"Start with a wedge and we'll work our way backward."

After examining the boy's grip and making some minor adjustments, Josh stepped away.

"Let's see you hit a few."

Her shoulders knotted with tension, Cari wrapped her arms around her updrawn knees. For the first few minutes, she jumped every time a metal club face connected with a ball. After each swing, she listened as nervously as Eric for Josh's feedback.

Gradually both she and the teenager relaxed. The teacher in her admired the way Josh minimized his criticism and maximized his praise every time a ball flew into the target.

"Good, good. You've got a nice even rhythm, but you need to follow through a little more. Forget about hitting the ball. You can't miss it."

"Wanna bet?" Eric muttered, scowling ferociously at the ball.

"Just think about hitting through it. Go right through it. That's it. Bring the club all the way over your shoulder. Good."

By the end of a half hour, ball after ball was flying at the target. Cari was grinning as broadly as Eric when Josh ended the lesson.

"This was awesome," the boy exclaimed. "I can't believe a little thing like hitting through the ball can make such a difference. Thanks, Josh."

"You're welcome."

Eric held out the club. "Here, I'll shag balls for you while you hit some."

"No thanks. I don't like using someone else's clubs."

"Granddad won't mind. Go ahead."

"Maybe later."

"Okay." Eric dropped the club into the bag with a thump and covered it with a protective cover. "I'll leave them here, under the awning, in case you decide to give them a try.''

He turned away, then spun back. "Hey, can we do this again tomorrow?"

"Sure."

"Great! I'm going to go tell Granddad what you taught me."

Cari smiled as Josh strolled over to her deck chair. "That's the most excited I've seen Eric on this trip."

Josh snagged a white towel from the back of his deck chair. "He's a good kid. And a good athlete."

"He's a better athlete now."

Swiping his face with a corner of the towel, Josh didn't reply for a moment. Perspiration trickled down the strong column of his neck and plastered his white knit shirt to his shoulders. His very broad and superbly muscled shoulders. Funny, Cari had never really noticed any symmetry or awesome physical beauty in the jocks who'd stumbled through her Western Civ classes. She couldn't seem to notice anything else around Josh.

"I didn't really teach him anything new," he replied at last. "Only reinforced a few basics."

"You reinforced a few basics for me, too."

He draped the towel around his neck and sent her one of those lazy, lopsided grins. "Is that so, Professor? Like what?"

"Like the fact that some instructors are born, not made. You're good, Josh. Very good."

His grin turned positively piratical. "When a beautiful woman tells me I've been good, I've usually been bad. Very bad. Want to go below and get bad together, Cari?"

He was doing it again. Deflecting discussion away from himself with a grin and a joke. Cari longed to beg him to stop, to share his real feelings with her. In the face of his refusal to let down his guard, she had no choice but to go along with his diversionary tactics. Pursing her lips, she sent him a minatory look from under the brim of her straw hat.

"I assume that's another version of getting naked and playing bride and groom."

"You assume correctly, Miss Prim."

She sniffed and reached for her tote bag. "Didn't you agree not to turn on the playboy charm? Why are you teasing me like this?"

When he didn't reply immediately, she glanced up. Awareness jolted through her like a high-voltage electrical current.

He wasn't teasing! He wanted to consummate their ridiculous marriage as much as she did. She could only assume that their imminent divorce held him back. As it did her.

Cari had done some crazy, impulsive things in her life. Walking out on her job had been one. Agreeing to participate in that silly marriage ceremony had been another. Those two minor catastrophes paled beside the idiocy she now gave in to.

Releasing her tote, she leaned across the short space between their chairs and framed Josh's face in her palms. His skin was hot and damp with sweat. And infinitely wonderful to her touch. She leaned closer, her hungry gaze on his mouth and her intentions written clearly across her face.

His hands came up to cup hers. "Cari. Sweetheart. This isn't smart."

"I know, but . . ."

"But what?"

"I think I need to kiss you, Josh."

"Need to?" His voice sounded harsh, ragged. "Or want to?"

"Both," she whispered as she brought her mouth to his.

He didn't move, didn't make any attempt to deepen the kiss. Cari didn't care. Within an instant, she was lost in her exploration of his taste and his scent and his feel. His lips were firm under hers. And warm. And wet on the slick inner skin of his mouth.

She might never taste him again, she reasoned while she could still think at all. After Cancún, she might never see him again.

She wanted only this.

Only a kiss.

Eight

It was only a kiss.

Crack!

A ball sailed toward the red blaze of the sun and slammed into the battered target. With savage satisfaction, Josh watched it bounce off the map and roll to the bottom of the net. He nudged another ball forward with his right foot.

Just a kiss.

Thwump!

The leading edge of the seven iron thunked into the carpet square, several inches short of the ball. Josh glared down at the white sphere, then lined up the iron once more.

One hell of a kiss.

Crack!

When the ball whipped into the target this time,

Josh's satisfaction was tempered by the realization that he'd missed as many times as he'd hit. And he was damned if he knew whether he owed his flawed aim to blurry vision or a lack of concentration.

Since the moment Cari's mouth had locked on his this morning, Josh hadn't been able to think of anything else. He'd been drum-tight all day. Now, with Saint Thomas's green peaks fading astern, and everyone else below decks resting before dinner, he'd come to the sun deck, desperate to release some of his pent-up physical frustration. There was no way he could have stayed in the cabin while Cari filled it with shower steam and the scent of lemony shampoo—not without ripping open the shower door and flattening her against the tiles.

Here, with only the sun and the sea and the privacy of his own thoughts, he could admit what had been simmering just below the level of his consciousness for days. He didn't want a divorce. Any more than he wanted this crazy marriage. He wanted...

Crack!

...to woo Cari. He wanted to tease her and flatter her and court her with silly gifts. He wanted to cage her against the boat rail and nibble at her throat. He wanted to go ashore and buy her a wedding ring, one she wouldn't slip off in a few days. Or a few years.

Thwump!

The club face slammed into the carpet square with a force that jarred Josh's wrists and arms all the way to the shoulder sockets.

Sure, Keegan, he told himself with a sneer. Sure. You want to offer Cari a happily-ever-after, when you don't even know whether you'll have an "after," happily or otherwise.

She had her future all planned out, in nice, neat increments. She'd finish her thesis. Get her doctorate. Move up through the professorial ranks. Maybe do a book about costuming through the ages.

He didn't know whether he'd be swinging a club or making motor-oil commercials a month from now. Whether he'd be the man he'd been until the accident, or someone altogether different. How could he ask Cari to commit to that someone when he didn't even know himself who he might be?

"What are you doing?"

He turned slowly, the seven iron loose in his hand. Cari hadn't showered. Hadn't changed. She still wore the white slacks and navy-blue T-shirt imprinted with a bust of Alexander the Great that she'd worn when they explored Saint Thomas this afternoon. Her hair drifted in soft, silky waves around her face, tinted to a deep gold by the late-afternoon sun.

"I thought I'd come up and knock off a few shots while you got ready for dinner."

"Dinner's not for an hour yet. It doesn't take me that long to shower and pull on my dress."

To Josh's consternation, she perched on the end of a deck chair and tucked her feet under her.

"I've never seen a golf game, or a pro golfer in action. Do you mind if I watch?"

That was all he needed. Thinking about Cari distracted him enough. Knowing she was perched just a few feet away while he duffed his shots certainly wouldn't improve his concentration.

"I've got a better idea. Why don't I give you your first golf lesson?"

"Me? No way! I wasn't kidding when I told Eric about remedial gym class."

"You can't be that bad."

"Trust me, I can."

He walked over to her, smiling a challenge. "You told me I was a good instructor. Maybe I can do better than... Who was it? Mrs. Lancaster?"

She held up both hands in protest. "No, Josh. Seriously, I have zero coordination. Less than zero. Twenty below zero."

Laughing, he caught one of her hands in his. "Come on, Cari. You might as well take something home from this cruise besides a sunburned nose and a scalded thigh."

She was. Cari's heart twisted with the silent admission. She was taking far more home from this cruise than she had ever dreamed she would. More than he would ever know. She was taking the memory of Josh's lip-tilted grin. The vivid image of his broad shoulders silhouetted against a gold Caribbean sun. The feel of his hand wrapped around hers.

Her palm brushed the ridge of calluses at the base of his fingers, calluses she now knew came from years of swinging a club. She'd never held a golf club in her life.

The feel of his toughened skin only emphasized how far apart their lives were. They inhabited totally different worlds. She with her books and her long-dead Tudors. He with his tournaments at places like Maui and Saint Andrews. For just a moment, just this one moment, Cari felt the urge to bridge their worlds, to share a little of his.

"Okay," she replied, letting him tug her off the deck chair. "I just hope you won't regret this."

"I won't."

"Mrs. Lancaster," she warned gloomily, "developed ulcers."

Cari hugged his rich, deep laughter to her chest like some precious gem.

"I'm not Mrs. Lancaster. I use a different instructional technique."

No kidding! As best Cari could recall, the high school gym teacher had never positioned her students parallel to a net, then wrapped her arms around them.

"Relax."

Sure. Uh-huh. She was supposed to relax, when Josh's hips were nudging her bottom and his breath was warming her left ear?

"Now hold out your hands, palms up."

He reached forward to lay the club in her palm. With the movement, more than his hips nudged Cari's bottom. Her face flamed an instant bright red as she once again pictured Josh in slashed doublet and tight hose, with his masculine attributes emphasized in the bold and bawdy Elizabethan manner.

"Just wrap your fingers around the shaft," he instructed.

Cari squirmed, her body heating as it touched his at a hundred different contact points. "I don't think this is going to work, Josh."

"Sure it is. Got a good grip? Okay, now look at the face of the club. See how it's lined up? Square to the ball, and to the trajectory you want it to follow?"

Gradually Josh's patience and teasing persistence drummed the basics of stance and swing into Cari. To her utter astonishment, she actually hit the ball on her first solo attempt. The fact that it ricocheted off the toe of the iron and sailed over the rail into the sea didn't lessen her amazement.

"I can't believe it! I hit it! Did you see that? I hit it!"

She swung around, ecstatic. Just in time, Josh ducked. The iron missed his head by inches.

"I saw it. Good shot." His hazel eye glinted with laughter. "Want to try another?"

"Sure." She thumped the carpet with the club and assumed a stance. "Think I can get this sucker in the net?"

She didn't get it in the net. She didn't get it anywhere near the net. In fact, she missed the ball completely and spun around in a full circle.

"Try again," Josh ordered.

Cari's euphoria took wing when she connected once again. This time the ball whizzed straight up in the air, came hurtling back down, bounced off the teak deck and splashed into the sea off the starboard rail.

Laughing, she twisted around to look over her shoulder. "I hope you've got a good supply of balls."

As soon as the words were out, she blushed brick red. Josh, of course, grinned wickedly.

"Don't worry. Just keep swinging."

She put a half dozen more into the sea before disaster stuck.

Cari was aiming for the net. She really was. She had no idea how the ball managed to cut ninety degrees to the left, hit the launch support, zing backward and smash into the radar dish mounted atop the flying bridge. She whirled around, eyes wide with dismay, as pieces of electrical components tinkled to the deck.

Josh bit his lip. "Maybe my instructional techniques aren't much better than Mrs. Lancaster's, after all."

Cari's horrified gaze was fixed on the shattered radar dish. "Do you think it can be fixed?"

"Replaced, maybe." He took the club from her limp grasp. "It's okay, Cari. It was an accident. Accidents happen in golf, just as they do in all other aspects of life."

His quiet comment helped Cari put the disaster in perspective. It took more than a quiet reply to defuse the captain's tight-lipped fury, however.

Paxton's anger took Cari by surprise. Until this point, the whiskered, weathered captain had displayed nothing but bluff affability. He wasn't the least affable or bluff as he marched out of the bridge and demanded to know what the hell was going on. Cari blinked at the lash in his voice, but refused to take refuge behind Josh's cool explanation of an impromptu golf lesson.

"Guess I hit an unlucky shot. I'm sorry, Captain."

"Unlucky?" Paxton almost spit out the word. "I'll say it was unlucky. Do you have any idea how expensive that piece of equipment is?"

"No, I don't," Cari replied, her chin lifting. "But I'll pay to repair or replace it, of course."

She tried to ignore the sinking sensation in the pit of her stomach. Replacing the radar dish would no doubt eat up what was left of her savings, and then some. Even with the grant, she'd have to work at least part-time to pay for the blasted thing. The chances of finishing her thesis within the deadline seemed more remote than ever before.

"If anyone's responsible for the damage, I am," Josh informed the captain coolly. "I took it on myself to instruct Cari, and I'll cover any costs your insurance doesn't."

Insurance! Of course! Cari heaved a huge sigh of relief. Prematurely, as it turned out.

"Cost isn't the problem," Paxton growled, plucking off his billed cap to slap it against his leg. "The problem is that we won't make it to Saint John. Not today, anyway. I'll have to turn back to Saint Thomas, locate a new dish and get it installed. That'll throw us off schedule by at least a day."

"I'll explain the delay to the other passengers," Josh replied. "I'm sure they'll be disappointed at missing Saint John and the pig roast, but we'll have another evening in Charlotte Amalie as consolation."

The captain slapped his cap against his leg again, muttering something under his breath about pig roasts that made Josh's eye narrow and Cari's widen.

Paxton caught their expressions and grimaced. "Sorry. I guess all old sea dogs get a little crusty when something happens to their ship. I'll get us headed back to Charlotte Amalie, then call the passengers together to announce the change."

Cari watched him stride away, still stiff with anger. "Whew! For a moment there, I thought he was going to tie me to the mast and drag out the cat-o'-nine-tails."

Josh didn't answer, his brows drawn together in a slashing frown as he watched the captain stride toward the bridge.

"Do you really think insurance will cover most of the cost?" Cari glanced up at the silent man beside her. "Josh?"

"What?"

She blinked, finding no trace of the laughing, teasing Josh of a few moments ago in this man's face. It was all hard planes and tight lines. She might be an uncoordinated klutz, but she wasn't stupid. Something other than a smashed radar dish was worrying him.

"What's the matter?"

"I'm not sure," he said slowly, his gaze flicking to the bridge once more. "I'm just trying to understand why our captain reacted so strongly to the idea of a change in schedule."

She chewed on her lower lip for a moment. "You're thinking that a man whose business depends on the whims of weather and the sea should be more flexible?"

"Something like that."

"Well, maybe he has to reserve anchorage in advance. Or take on supplies at certain specified points."

"Like diesel fuel," Josh murmured.

"Right."

"That could be it," he said thoughtfully.

At that moment, the *Nautilus III* began a slow, banking turn. Josh glanced beyond Cari at the island in the distance, and made a visible effort to shrug off the unpleasantness of the past few moments.

"The change in schedule might have put a dent in Captain Paxton's mood, but we won't let it ruin ours. Why don't we go ashore for dinner tonight?"

"Just you and me?"

"Just you and me."

"No Eric?"

"No Eric. No Evelyn and Paul. No anybody but us."

Ever afterward, memories of that night could bring a dreamy smile to Cari's mouth. Hopeless romantic that she was, she gloried in the idyllic setting and her dashing companion.

In crisp tan slacks and a blue cotton shirt with the sleeves rolled up to reveal tanned, muscular forearms, he radiated casual sophistication. The black eye patch only added to his rakish male charm. Cari felt her heart pound out an erratic beat as he tucked her hand in the crook of his arm and led her to the outboard stairs.

Enrique's dark eyes skimmed over Josh, then settled on Cari. "So, you go ashore? Just you and your man?"

Her face heated at his casual use of the possessive. "Yes, just us."

Ignoring Enrique's offer of help, Josh handed her into the launch himself. He sat beside her on the center seat and looped a casual arm around her waist while the steward steered the small boat through brilliant, shifting bands of aquamarine, lapis lazuli and sapphire toward Charlotte Amalie's main pier.

"What time do you want me to come back?" Enrique asked, steadying the launch as Josh helped Cari onto the pier.

"We'll call the ship when we're ready."

They followed the curving waterfront street lined with three-story pink-and-white buildings, and it seemed as natural as breathing for Cari to take the hand Josh held out to her. Together they peered down narrow alleys, strolled under intricate archways erected by the Danes who had originally settled the island and admired the fancy grillwork that added such architectural character to the city.

Cari wasn't blind to the fact that Josh garnered as much admiration as the architecture. More than one female head turned for another look at his tall, athletic frame. If he caught any of the glances sent his way, he didn't show it. His attention stayed wholly and exclusively on Cari. As a result, she felt just like Maria in *West Side Story*—pretty and witty and wise. Incredibly so.

She might have acquired her mint-green V-necked cotton tunic and long, matching jacquard print skirt on sale several years ago, but Cari didn't feel the least obligation to tell Josh that. Especially not when he complimented her on the color and mentioned that it brought out the sunshine in her hair.

Nor did she protest when he tugged her toward a taxi stand and answered her inquiries about where they were headed with a shrug and a grin. All he would tell her during the twenty-minute ride was that the spot he was taking her to was special.

It was.

So special that Cari gasped when she stepped out of the taxi onto the high, windswept promontory known as Drake's Seat. An ornate wooden sign proclaimed that the English privateer had once climbed to this very spot and watched treasure-laden galleons of every flag sail through the passage he himself had first navigated in 1580.

"Oh, Josh! I don't believe it! I'm standing where Sir Francis Drake once stood!"

The tanned skin at the corner of Josh's mouth crinkled. "I thought that might thrill your little Elizabethan soul."

"How did you know about this place?"

"Paul Sanders mentioned it to me while I was giving Eric his lesson this morning. Said he'd tried to talk Evelyn into driving up here to see the view, but couldn't pry her out of the shops."

"Can you imagine anyone passing this up?"

Awed by the panoramic view of the U.S. and British Virgin Islands caught in the slanting rays of the setting sun, Cari spun in a slow circle. For a few heartbeats, it seemed as though time and space were compressed to this single instant.

She was breathing in the same air, viewing the same spectacular scene, as those long-ago seafarers. She could almost hear the distant crack of sails and shouts of sailors as they strained at the ropes. Almost feel their excitement as they spotted a rich prize trying to slip through the passage. Never had history come so alive for her.

She closed her eyes and breathed it into her pores. Then she turned to Josh, smiling.

"Thank you."

"You're welcome."

His answering smile pierced the mists of time and gave Cari a glimpse of her future. No matter what happened in Cancún, she knew she would hold this special place and this very special man in her heart forever.

She'd once called him an oversexed, overmuscled jock. Yet he'd given her a gift more precious to her than diamonds. He'd understood her passion for history and brought her here to share it. Josh Keegan possessed more sensitivity, more innate respect for her as a person, than Dr. Edward Grant ever had.

The thought humbled Cari . . . and made her realize that her vow to swear off all men from now until the next millennium might have been a bit hasty. Sometime in the past few days she'd come perilously close to tumbling into love with a man she hardly knew.

The realization sobered her, and gave her the courage to ask the questions she'd shied away from until this point.

She waited until they were ensconced in huge straw plantation chairs on the verandah of the Mountain Top restaurant. Sipping her banana daiquiri, Cari let Josh order for them both. For the moment, she was content to watch the breeze ruffle his dark hair and listen to the counterpoint of his deep voice against the bright beat of the island music coming from inside the restaurant. Their conversation drifted while they waited for dinner, ranging from treasure-laden galleons and privateers to the history of this string of islands.

"Columbus landed here on his second voyage," Cari related as the waiter deposited huge platters of succulent sea bass smothered in fried plantains in front of them. "Supposedly he named these islands for the followers of Saint Ursula."

"Her followers all being virgins, I suppose?"

"All eleven thousand of them," Cari replied primly. "According to legend, at least."

Josh choked on a forkful of sea bass. "Eleven thousand virgins! No wonder these islands were overrun with rogues and brigands. They were all probably looking for a few of Saint Ursula's followers."

Never one to gloss over historical fact, Cari made a face. "Among other things. Both the people and the lands in this part of the world were systematically raped in the mindless quest for treasure."

"Sounds like another good topic for a paper. Maybe you should research it when you get home."

"Mmm...maybe. I'll have plenty of research to keep me busy as it is when I get home."

She hesitated, then decided to use the opening he'd given her. "What about you, Josh? What are you going to do when you get back to the States?"

His mouth curved in the beginning of a crooked grin, and Cari held up a quick hand.

"Don't! Please, don't turn me off with a smile and a joke," she pleaded softly. "Not tonight."

His grin didn't make it to full power. For long moments, he searched her eyes.

"I don't know what I'm going to do," he said finally.

"What about golf?"

"I don't know, Cari."

For a moment, she thought that was all he was going to say. Disappointment washed through her in rolling waves. Then he began to trace an aimless pattern on the table with his fork. Slowly, hesitantly, he shared a small part of himself with her.

"Golf is all I know. My dad started taking me out on Sunday mornings before I was big enough to know which end of a club was up. I was a PGA junior prospect in high school, and went through college on a golf scholarship. It's more than a game to me, Cari. It's an avocation. A way of life. Or it was."

The fork stilled, and he met her gaze.

"The doctors don't know when, if ever, I'll regain my full sight. Or my balance. So I'll have to learn to compensate in my swing. Or find another way to make a living."

"Can you do it? Compensate, I mean?"

"I don't know."

There wasn't a trace of self-pity or desperation in his quiet reply, but Cari's throat ached. Then he slanted her a glinting look that was all Josh.

"Actually, I had just made up my mind to find out what I could and couldn't do the night of the charity ball. Then I got distracted by a gorgeous woman in a... What did you call that contraption? A farthingale?"

And by an unscheduled wedding, Cari thought. He'd had the accident to deal with, and then he'd put his life on hold once again while he took care of the little matter of their divorce. Yet he refused to wallow in his problems. He wasn't that kind of man. In keeping with his swashbuckling image, he smiled and joked and turned the subject away from himself and his uncertain future. But Cari knew now that her pirate's buckle didn't swash quite as much as he wanted everyone to believe.

"A farthingale," she confirmed, her throat still tight.

"Hmm... I wonder what Saint Ursula would have thought of Queen Juana's invention?"

His teasing question flowed into a lively debate on the possibility of eleven thousand virgins.

Cari followed his lead, acknowledging the inescapable fact that Josh's easy banter and playboy facade disguised a complex, intelligent man with old-fashioned values. He didn't air his personal concerns in public. He didn't ask for help with them. And, she admitted with an inner sigh, he didn't seduce women.

He hadn't seduced her, anyway.

For all his teasing about getting naked and getting bad, he hadn't made any attempt to take advantage of their awkward situation. He hadn't even followed up on her kiss this morning. Funny, she'd thought that kiss would be enough for her to hold in her heart after the cruise. She knew now it wasn't. Not anywhere near enough.

She wanted more. The feel of his skin slick against hers. The whisper of his laughter in her ear. The scent of his lovemaking on her body. She wanted Josh.

They were married, her heart argued fiercely. For a few more days, at least, they were husband and wife. Why shouldn't they enjoy the privileges that came with marriage before they divorced? Why shouldn't they bring the attraction sizzling between them to a flashpoint?

Cari slanted the man across the table from her a slow, assessing look. Darn it, why wouldn't Josh live up to his bad-boy image, just this once?

Obviously, if there was going to be any ravishing done, she'd have to do it herself.

Nine

—

Cari tugged the hem of her sleep shirt down over her hips. As nightgowns went, the T-shirt was designed more for comfort than for seduction. Since she hadn't brought anything more alluring with her, however, it would have to do. Giving her freshly brushed hair and scrubbed face a final glance in the bathroom mirror, she opened the door and stepped into the master suite.

Josh glanced up, his fingers working the buttons of his blue shirt. "Done?"

Cari drew in a deep breath. "Not quite. Before you go into the bathroom and we settle into our separate beds for the night, there's something I think you should know."

"What? You used up all the toothpaste?"

"I want to play games with you, Josh. Bride and groom. Pirate and lady. Anything but golf."

His fingers stilled on the buttons as he stared at Cari in astonishment. "You want to do what?"

She drifted toward him, her bare feet digging into the pale carpet. She'd thought about her approach all the way back to the ship. She wasn't a world-class expert in this seduction business, by any means, but she was woman enough to recognize her strengths—and her weaknesses. Josh definitely fit into the latter category. Just looking at him now made her toes curl into the carpet.

She'd classify her ability to face things head-on as a decided strength, though. So she'd decided to sail in with all guns blazing, like the pirates of old. She stopped in front of him, and her heart was pounding as she fired her next salvo.

"I want to get naked with you," she said softly. "I want to get bad. Very bad. Or was it good?" She bit her lip. "Whatever."

"Whatever?" He stared down at her, still stunned.

"I want to love you," she whispered, her fingers brushing his aside as she reached for the shirt buttons. "Tonight. Tomorrow. Until we reach Cancún."

His hands closed over hers. "Cari..."

"I know, I know," she said fiercely, interrupting him. "This isn't smart. Any smarter than the kiss this afternoon. But we're...we're on our honeymoon, Josh. For the next few days, at least, we're on our honeymoon. We're not supposed to think about the future. We're not supposed to think about anything but right here and right now."

Despite her determination to carry on as boldly and bawdily as any of her beloved Tudors, she might have lost her nerve right then, if she hadn't caught the tiny tic in one side of Josh's jaw. And felt the jackhammer of his heartbeat under her fingertips. Emboldened, she tugged her hands free of his and unbuttoned the last button. Sliding her palms inside his shirt, she spread it open.

"Don't worry about tomorrow or the day after," she murmured. "They'll take care of themselves. Just think about the fact that I want to kiss you. Right now. And right here."

Leaning forward, she planted her mouth on the warm, taut skin of his chest. To her absolute delight, a muscle jumped under her lips, and his pulse accelerated from fast to furious. Glancing up a few breathless moments later, she caught a soft, warning glint in his eye.

"You're playing a dangerous game here, sweetheart. Sure you know the rules?"

"I'm making them up as I go."

"Well, I just might have a few of my own."

He reached for her, but she slipped his shirt off his shoulders and drew it down his arms. It hooked at his elbows, trapping his arms at his sides.

"You had your chance to have your way with me, Keegan," she teased in a low, husky voice. "Several times, in fact. Now it's my turn."

"Is that so?"

"That's so. You're my prisoner, big guy. I intend to do all kinds of evil things to you." She nipped at his chest to emphasize her point, then licked the small spot.

"Christ, Cari!"

His muscles had tensed to solid steel. All of them, she noted with a fierce, singing satisfaction as she pressed herself against him. Josh might be too much of a gentleman to seduce her and complicate their already absurd situation, but he wasn't exactly adverse to being seduced. He wanted her. As much as she wanted him. For tonight. For tomorrow.

That was enough, she told herself fiercely. That was all she was asking for.

Urgent need swept through Cari, more urgent than any she'd ever felt. She didn't want to waste a moment of their time together. Her hands slid up his arms, memorizing the slope of smooth muscle, the curve of corded skin. Her fingers locked behind his neck.

She took her time with the kiss. And her pleasure. Her mouth moved over his in slow, sensual exploration. As he had this morning, Josh held himself still, letting her test the silky skin of his inner lip. The sharp edge of his teeth. She pulled his head down, slanting hers to gain greater access. He gave her only what she demanded, but his skin rippled with the effort of holding back.

So he intended to play along with her little game. Pretend he was her prisoner. Let her have her way with him. Shivery excitement pulsed through Cari at the thought of shedding the restraints of her own shyness and doing everything she wanted to—and with—Josh.

Burying her hands in his hair, Cari raised up on tiptoe and put her overflowing need into her kiss. Her hands roamed his chest, his shoulders. His hips rocked into hers. When she leaned back, her pulse raced at the answering raw need she saw in his face.

"At this point," she murmured between ragged breaths, "I think I'm supposed to sweep you off your feet and carry you to bed. Do you suppose we could skip the carrying part and go straight to bed?"

"Not a chance," he replied, with a slow, wicked grin that made Cari's already erratic pulse skip a half-dozen beats. "We'll just reverse roles a bit."

In an instant, he had snaked a hand free of the confining shirtsleeves and wrapped an arm around her waist. His other hand delved beneath her cotton tunic to find the elastic of her panties. The feel of his fingers on her bare skin shocked Cari into even more heightened awareness.

"Josh!"

"It's too late for protests, sweetheart. Way too late."

He proceeded to strip her with a speed and an unerring skill that made Cari squeak and squirm. With some chagrin, she revised her earlier assessment about Josh's bad-boy image. It wasn't, she decided, such a facade after all. She was naked and laughing and blushing furiously from head to toe when he swooped her up in his arms.

"Now, my lusty little Elizabethan, prepare to meet your fate."

He strode to the bed, his prize in his arms. Somewhere between the middle of the room and the huge bed, however, Cari lost the urge to laugh and Josh lost the urge to play any more games.

When he lowered her to the satin coverlet a few seconds later, he was ready, more than ready, to get bad. Or good. Or whatever. When she held out her arms to him, it took all Josh had not to follow her down to the bed.

"Wait, Cari. Wait a moment."

She lay still, her heart slamming against her ribs. He was back a moment later, a foil packet in his hand and a stark hunger on his face that made her womb clench. When he sheathed himself and turned to her, Cari opened her arms and her heart.

With the grace and beauty and solid strength of a natural athlete, Josh fit himself into them. Gasping, she arched her hips while he settled his solid weight between her legs. His teeth and tongue played with her turgid nipples. His hand explored her slick, hot core.

Fierce, male satisfaction flowed through Josh at the feel of her wet heat. Suckling and nipping, he feasted on the breasts he'd fantasized about since the moment he'd first spotted them about to pop out of her gown, until she was writhing and groaning under him.

Frantic to return the exquisite pleasure that streaked through her body, Cari slid her palms down his ribs, his waist, his hips. Her fingers closed around his rigid shaft. Her last thought, while she could still think at all, was that Josh definitely didn't need any padding to fill out his doublet and tights.

Moments, or maybe hours, later, he thrust into her. She forgot about sixteenth-century costuming. She forgot about their twentieth-century dilemma. She forgot to think, to touch, to breathe. She could only lift her hips in instinctive response, and follow where he led. With each stroke of his hips against her, Cari soared higher. And tighter. And longer.

With every spasm of her muscles around him, Josh felt his control slip a little more. His muscles rigid, his blood on fire, he took her mouth once more. Then she took him. To a fiery, spiraling plane of red heat and white light.

Arching under him, she gave a raw groan and climaxed. Long, splintering moments later, Josh did, too.

They lay entwined, panting, sweating. Then he rolled over and fit her into the curve of his body. Quiet, lazy moments followed. Cari breathed in the scent of her body mingled with his, and then discovered an entirely new aspect to lovemaking.

"Kind of sad, isn't it?" he murmured, nuzzling her hair.

Startled, she drew back to peer up at him. "Sad?"

She could think of a hundred, a thousand, different adjectives to describe what had just happened between them. *Sad* wasn't one of them.

He planted a kiss on her nose. "About those eleven thousand virgins. Just look what they missed."

Sputtering with laughter, she burrowed into his warmth and made a surprising discovery. This cuddling and teasing after sexual release were more erotic, more intimate, than the physical act itself. Still, a deep, feminine part of her thrilled when he hardened against her once again. Boldly she rolled him over and straddled his hips.

Her store of boldness wore out long before Josh's energy did. Boneless and exhausted, she made no protest when he dragged her sleep shirt over her head and tucked her firmly into the curve of his body. She fell asleep with her head on his shoulder and a single thought drifting through her dazed mind. *This* was what a honeymoon was all about, this laughter and passion and joy.

* * *

The slam of a solid object against his chest yanked Josh awake some hours later. He gave a startled grunt and jerked upright, his sluggish senses trying to identify the source of the attack. Wide-eyed and staring, he searched the cabin, still dimly lit by the lights they'd left on earlier.

"Eleven thousand!" Cari muttered fiercely, flinging out an arm.

This time, she caught him squarely in the stomach. He grunted again, then his attacker flopped over and buried her face in her pillow.

Rubbing his stomach, Josh grinned ruefully and laid back down. A heavy leg over hers kept them from scissoring. More or less. His arm reached around her waist to pin her body against his. Her small, rounded breast shaped itself to his palm. His fingers played with her tender flesh under its covering of soft cotton.

She grumbled in her sleep and pushed her bottom into his groin in an unconscious effort to free herself.

"Oh, no, my lady," he murmured, his breath stirring the fine, fair hair tangled around her face. "You're not getting away from me again. Ever."

As soon as the whispered words were out, Josh knew he meant them. To his surprise, the tension he'd carried deep within him for the past few months loosened. Just a little. One small twist of the wire-tight coil. But loosen it did.

He tucked Cari closer against his body.

All these weeks, he'd worried about whether he'd be able to play pro golf again. In the past few hours, he'd come to accept that there were more important things in life than striding into the winner's circle at Augusta to slip on the green Master's jacket. Like playing silly sex games with Cari. And watching her face light up when history came alive in front of her eyes. And holding her breast in his hand while she muttered and wiggled in her sleep.

For the first time, Josh faced the fact that he might not ever play his sport again with something less than quiet desperation. The idea of hawking golf shoes for a living or hosting a string of functions as celebrity spokesman for the physically challenged still caused a tight knot in his stomach, but the prospect didn't dismay him as much as it had before.... Before Cari.

He shifted a little, glancing down at her face. She frowned at his movement and mumbled irritably in her sleep. At her annoyed pout, Josh felt the coiled tension loosen another twist.

Funny, he'd never thought of love this way. This slow easing of doubts and uncertainties. This growing conviction that he wanted to share the rest of his nights with a grumpy bed partner in perpetual motion.

Lost in his thoughts, Josh didn't realize for some time that not all the movement in the cabin came from Cari. Some of the bed's quivering was caused by the yacht's engines. He lifted his head a few inches, listening to the muted sounds of the anchor winching up. A moment later, he felt a slow up-and-down rocking motion as the *Nautilus III* nosed around and got under way.

Josh eased back down, stilling Cari's annoyed twitch with a tight hold and a soft kiss. Paxton hadn't wasted much time getting the replacement radar up and operational, he mused. When Enrique picked them up at the pier tonight, he'd confirmed that the captain had tracked down a radar dish at one of Charlotte Amalie's many boatyards. An older model, the steward had informed Josh and Cari with a shrug, but reliable.

Evidently the new radar wasn't as reliable as Enrique had indicated, Josh decided some hours later. Always a light sleeper, he came awake again at the muted sound of a man's shout, followed immediately by sudden silence as the engines shut down. In the stillness, Josh thought he caught Paxton's gruff curse.

A quick glance at the dark outline behind the curtains showed that it was early, not yet dawn. Not wanting Cari exposed to another dose of the captain's temper, Josh decided to go topside and defuse the situation as best he could.

When he slid his shoulder from under her cheek, she twitched and muttered and scrunched her body into a tight ball, but didn't wake. Smiling, Josh pulled on his gray sweats and a pair of canvas deck shoes. A few moments later, he let himself out of the cabin.

He made his way noiselessly along the narrow walkway toward the stairs leading to the sun deck, steadying himself with a hand on the rail. The polished wood deck lifted and fell beneath his feet. The sea was choppy just before dawn, Josh realized. Either that, or they were in for some weather.

He took the stairs to the sun deck and headed for the starboard side walkway to the bridge, only to stop abruptly. Eye narrowed, he took in the scene illuminated by dimmed ship lights.

Josh's first thought was that the trawler tied amidships to the *Nautilus III* by thick lines bow and stern belonged to Paxton's shady supplier. A second, closer look revealed that the smaller craft wasn't supplying the yacht with bootlegged diesel fuel.

Josh's jaw tightened when he spotted the netted, unmarked crates being winched aboard the *Nautilus*. He was willing to bet those wooden boxes contained another form of contraband entirely, one that would explain a lot of things. Like the ridiculously low cost of this cruise, even when offered as a prize. The fact that the captain was as anxious as Josh to avoid a flotilla of paparazzi trailing his ship. His nervousness and spurt of temper when he'd thought he'd missed his contact off Saint John.

With a slow twisting in his gut, Josh guessed that he and Cari and the rest of the passengers were along to serve as window dressing while the captain engaged in some very profitable and very dangerous smuggling.

Dammit, he should have realized that Paxton's willingness to keep their honeymoon under wraps was too good to be true. The man could have made a fortune with a single phone call to the tabloids. The cargo he was taking on now had to be worth more. A whole lot more. Which made the situation Josh now found himself in dangerous as hell.

"Careful, cousin! Careful!"

At the urgent, low-voiced command, Josh flattened himself against the bulkhead. A few yards forward, Enrique stretched over the rail to grab at the wildly swinging net. Seconds later, the trawler thumped into the side of the yacht and Paxton joined the steward at the rail.

"For God's sake, Salazar!" he hissed to the man at the wheel of the bobbing trawler. "Can't you control that damn tuna bucket?"

Paxton's business partner lifted a hand from the wheel and sent an obscene gesture across the waves.

Enrique grunted and hauled the netted cargo onto the forward deck. While he stooped to release the winch line from the net, Paxton and the other captain verified times and contacts for pickup of the cargo in Miami.

Josh stayed plastered to the bulkhead and listened intently, memorizing the details. Not that he dared do anything else. He was well outside the circle of hazy gray cast by the other boat's mast light, but he didn't want to risk moving and catching Salazar's attention.

With jaws so tight they ached, he kept completely still while Enrique tossed the heavy lines down into the trawler. Its engines chugging in the predawn darkness, the battered fishing boat pulled away.

When the circle of light had faded in the distance, Josh started to inch his way back toward the sun deck. He'd almost made it when a thin, gangly figure materialized on the walkway.

"Hey, Josh!"

Eric's reedy voice split the darkness. Josh cursed viciously under his breath and sliced a hand through the air to still the boy. Either the teenager didn't see the gesture or he ignored it.

"Did that thump against the side of the boat wake you up, too? It hit right beside my bunk."

"Eric, get below."

"What was it?" the boy asked, his bare feet slapping the deck as he moved forward. "A shark or something? Did you see it?"

Josh cursed again as another set of footsteps sounded behind him. He turned to find Paxton's eyes narrowed to slits in his whiskered face and his fist wrapped around a lethal-looking handgun. Enrique stood just behind him, his mouth twisted with fear.

One look at the captain's eyes told Josh he didn't have a prayer of convincing these men that he hadn't witnessed the exchange. All he could do was try to save the boy. Keeping his body between Eric and the gun, Josh held the captain's eyes.

"It was a dolphin," he replied, turning only his head to the boy.

"Cool!"

"It swam away, though. There's nothing to see now. You'd better go back to your cabin before your grandparents wake and start to worry."

"A typhoon couldn't wake them," the boy scoffed. "Granddad is sawing Zs big-time and Gram is . . ."

"Get below, kid!"

The captain's sharp command brought the teen up short. Frowning, he looked to Josh.

"Go below, Eric. It's too early to be up."

"Oh, yeah? What about you?"

Josh ground his back teeth. *If* he got out of this, and *if* he convinced Cari to extend their honeymoon indefinitely, and *if* they ever had kids, he sincerely hoped they could bypass the Eric stage.

"I needed some air. I'll head back down when I get through talking to Captain Paxton. Go on, now."

As the teenager made his way back to the sun deck, the three men faced each other. In the taut silence, Josh could hear Eric's bare feet slapping against the deck, then the stairs. When the echo of his steps faded, Enrique broke the stillness.

"What will we do with him, Captain? Shoot him? Break his neck and throw him overboard?"

Paxton uttered a filthy curse. "You idiot! Then his wife reports him missing, and the Coast Guard and the damned navy swarm all over us. Not to mention every reporter on two continents. Shut up and let me think."

"The Medellín, they will not like this."

"Shut up, I said!"

"The Medellín," Josh echoed, his brow lifting. "You're playing with the big boys, Paxton."

"Too big to cross, Keegan."

Without seeming to, Josh measured the distance between himself and the captain. One good kick, and he could send the gun into the sea. Maybe. Josh didn't even consider promising to keep silent. He wasn't the kind of man to make deals with drug smugglers, and he knew damn well Paxton wouldn't take his word for it anyway.

The captain's next words confirmed that fact.

"I'm not a killer, Keegan. But we're talking a lot of money here. A lot. I think you're going to have to drop out of circulation for a few days. You and your wife."

The knot in Josh's gut tightened. He tensed his muscles for the kick, trying desperately to line up the gun in a darkness made even fuzzier by his blurred vision.

"You're on the last leg of your honeymoon. No one's going to think it too strange if you and the missus want to enjoy every moment of it. By the time you two come up for air, we'll have off-loaded our cargo. We can decide what to do about you then." He waved the gun in the direction of the sun deck. "Get moving."

Josh didn't fool himself. Paxton might not be a killer, but the Colombian drug lords he was in business with were.

He waited until the captain had taken a step closer, concentrated fiercely on the dim outline of the weapon in Paxton's hand, then swung his foot in a vicious arc.

The mattress dipped suddenly.

The abrupt movement pierced Cari's deep, sleepy fog. Not ready to wake up, she raised her arms to drag the pillow over her head. Or tried to. To her consternation, she couldn't move them. A heavy form weighted the covers wrapped around her and kept her pinned solidly to the bed.

Josh.

She lay still for a moment, letting memories of the night before drift into her mind. With them came a delicious heat.

Never, ever, had she imagined that making love could be such a glorious, shattering experience. Or that she could let go of all her inhibitions and tickle and tease and torment a man like that. No, not *a* man. She could never have played those kinds of games with her former fiancé, old what's-his-name. Only with Josh. Wicked, grinning, incredibly gentle Josh.

She tried to move once more. After a small, futile struggle, she discovered in some astonishment that her arms weren't pinned by the covers. They were tied! Behind her back!

Her face blazed with heat. This went beyond the kind of games she was willing to play, even with...

"So you wake, eh?"

With some effort, Cari twisted her head. Her jaw sagged when she saw Enrique standing beside the bed. She blinked again. Several times. He didn't disappear.

A muffled grunt sounded behind her back. She gave Enrique another astonished look, then twisted furiously in the confining sheets. A startled cry rose in her throat at the sight of Josh sitting next to her, his back to the headboard and his arms twisted behind him.

"Oh, my God! Josh, are you all right?"

The question was rather pointless, since the gag in his mouth prevented an answer, but Cari wasn't thinking too clearly at this point.

"Not so pretty now, your man, is he?"

Cari ignored the sneer in Enrique's voice as her shocked gaze took in Josh's battered face. It looked awful. Worse than awful. Like something a zookeeper might feed to a hungry lion. Dried blood crusted his split lip. A huge, purpling bruise spread across one cheekbone. His eye, his one good eye, was swollen and puffy and as colorful as a winter gourd.

She fought to keep her sudden panic out of her voice as she twisted back to face Enrique. "What happened? What's going on?" Despite her best efforts, her voice quavered. "Why are we tied up?"

"Because your husband, he is a fool."

His mouth twisted, and for the first time Cari noticed the battle marks on his face, as well.

"He thinks to take us both, me and the captain. He is a fool."

"The captain?" Cari squeaked in dismay. "Is he part of this, too? Whatever this is?"

Ignoring her panicky questions, Enrique reached for her bound arms. He dragged her upright and propped her against the headboard, then bent to loop the end of a thick rope through the bedframe.

"Hey!" Cari sputtered in helpless protest. "What's going on here? Why are you—ooopf!"

Her face scrunched in distaste as the burly steward shoved a wadded washcloth into her mouth, then quickly secured it in place with one of Josh's ties.

When he lifted an ugly-looking gun from the table beside the bed, Cari's eyes widened. Stark, unreasoning fear swelled her chest, almost choking her. Then Enrique tucked the weapon into his waistband and rocked back on his heels, surveying them both with savage satisfaction.

"I will come back later. With food, perhaps. We'll see what the captain says. In the meantime, you will enjoy your honeymoon, yes?"

Ten

The minutes dragged past, one after another. Gradually Cari's heart stopped pumping terror through her veins. Slowly her panic subsided to mere fear. After a while, a creeping indignation overtook fear.

This was *not* her idea of a vacation—or a honeymoon!

She squirmed sideways to face Josh, trying to figure out what in the world had happened. His battered face gave her no clue. Nor did his muffled grunts and jerky movements. Realizing he was trying to wriggle free of his bonds, she went to work on her own.

She gave up ten agonizing minutes later, her wrists burning. Enrique had tied sailor's knots that defied any landlubber's ability to unravel them. Josh struggled on long after Cari gave up, but eventually he grunted in disgust and leaned his head back against the tall, padded headboard.

At that point, several unrelated but equally disturbing bits of information infiltrated her consciousness. One, she wore her sleep shirt, but her panties lay on the carpet halfway across the suite. Two, the feel of Josh's hair-roughened leg rubbing hers gave her a fierce, irrational courage. Three, she had to go to the bathroom.

The minutes ticked by. Bright light streamed in under the drawn curtains. Cari's stomach rumbled. Josh rubbed her leg encouragingly.

An hour passed. Maybe two. Cari's hands felt numb. The wadded washcloth left a taste of soap in her mouth. She had to go to the bathroom. Badly.

Later, she fumed, obviously had a different meaning to Enrique from the rest of the world.

Her physical discomfort grew to such dramatic proportions that by the time the steward finally returned, Cari's panic had little to do with the gun tucked in the waistband of his white slacks. He set a tray on the mahogany table and strolled over to her side of the bed. Bruises stood out like purple pansies against the skin around his left eye.

"I will untie your gag and then your hands, yes? But you will not scream, or I must hurt you. You or your man. You understand?"

Cari nodded.

"Good. Lean forward."

His big paws fumbled at the tie holding the washcloth in place. When it came free, Cari spit the cloth out and swallowed furiously to get some moisture into her dry mouth.

"Now I will free your hands and you will eat." He shot Josh a malevolent glance. "Then, perhaps, I will let you feed your man."

Cari gasped as the ropes around her wrists came free. Her arms dropped forward, sending needles of fire through her shoulder sockets.

"Eat now, and quickly."

She slid off the bed, tugging her sleep shirt down over her thighs. With some effort, she pulled her ravaged dignity around her like a cloak.

"Before I eat," she announced with a calm that amazed her, "I have to attend to my personal needs."

Enrique frowned at her for a moment, then curled his lip. "I must come with you, you understand."

To Cari's intense relief, the steward followed her into the bathroom, but not into the small private stall. Relief turned to frustration, however, when she found nothing more lethal than a toilet-paper holder in the tiny cubicle.

She emerged some moments later. Snagging her robe from the hook on the back of the bathroom door, she dragged it on. Then she grabbed a clean washcloth, dampened it in the sink and marched back into the bedroom, Enrique at her heels.

Throughout the short excursion, Cari searched frantically for something to disable Enrique with. She considered trying to spray her astringent lemon facial cleanser into his eyes, but quickly abandoned that idea as too risky. Somehow, she didn't think the cleanser would incapacitate him sufficiently for her to seize his weapon.

A moment later, her hand closed around the thermal coffeepot on the tray. The hot liquid had certainly disabled her for a few moments.

Unfortunately, Enrique stayed well across the suite while she forced herself to eat a dry croissant and a banana. He moved closer when she carried the tray to the bed to feed Josh, but only enough to let the bound man see the gun trained at her right temple.

"You will not shout, Keegan. Not unless you wish harm to your wife."

Cari struggled with the tie knotted around Josh's neck for some moments. When it gave, she eased the cloth out of his mouth. He swallowed convulsively, then sipped at the coffee she held to the unbruised corner of his mouth.

"What's going on?" she asked quietly.

Josh glanced at Enrique. When the steward didn't warn him to keep silent, chills raced down Josh's spine. Apparently what Cari knew or didn't know would make little difference to her fate.

"I took a walk topside early this morning," he told her. "Too early, as it turns out."

While she dabbed at his lip with a dampened cloth, he related what had happened. When he mentioned the drugs and Eric's intrusion on the scene, Cari paled.

"He's okay," Josh assured her quickly. "He went below before things got . . . messy."

The hand holding the cloth began to shake, and Josh cursed under his breath. He made no attempt to gloss over their situation, however. Cari had a right to know the danger she faced. When he finished, she gripped the damp cloth in both hands and swiveled to face Enrique.

"You can't really mean to keep us in this cabin for the rest of the trip? Four whole days? The other passengers will certainly question our absence."

Enrique shrugged, avoiding her eyes. "Perhaps not four more days. You could decide to leave the boat in Grand Cayman."

Josh stiffened, and water dripped from the cloth Cari wrung in her hands.

"Leave the boat?" she echoed faintly.

"To extend your honeymoon on this most pleasant island, you understand? We drop anchor there late this afternoon." He waved the gun in a small circle. "Now feed your man, and hurry. I have things I must do."

Josh's heart ached at the expression in her eyes when she turned back to him.

"I'm sorry, Cari."

"This isn't your fault."

"Yes, it is. I talked you into that crazy wedding. If it weren't for me, you wouldn't be on this damned honeymoon cruise . . . or in this mess."

By imperceptible degrees, the stark fear in her eyes receded. To Josh's utter amazement, she managed a wobbly smile.

"I admit I may have acted impulsively a time or two in my life. And I may have done some things I later regretted. Honeymooning with you isn't one of them, Josh."

He opened his mouth to reply, but Enrique's brusque demand for them to hurry preempted him. She broke off one end of the croissant and held it to his mouth. Taking the bite she offered, he chewed a couple of times, then swallowed slowly.

"I love you, Cari."

The strain in her face gave way to an expression he knew he'd keep tucked in his heart for the rest of his life, however long or short that might be.

"That's good," she replied softly. "Because I love you, too."

He grinned, and she popped another bite into his mouth.

Enrique departed soon afterward, leaving Cari and Josh securely bound and gagged once more. The lock clicked audibly in the stillness.

Before the echo had died away, Josh went to work on the ropes again. He was damned if he was going to let Paxton and company hurt his wife. He had hoped he and Cari would have time, a day or two at least, to come up with an escape plan. According to Enrique, they only had until this afternoon.

Grimly he twisted his wrists and sawed the ropes back and forth against the corner of the headboard. The friction scored his already raw skin. Josh ignored the sticky blood trickling down his clenched fists.

He was concentrating so fiercely on his task that the movement on the far side of the huge bed barely registered in his peripheral vision. But he couldn't fail to notice when Cari swung her arms up and yanked the gag out of her mouth.

Wrists dripping blood, he watched in utter stupefaction as she crawled across the bed and reached for his gag. Seconds later, he spit the cloth out.

"How the hell did you do that?"

"I bent my wrists when Enrique tied me this time," she panted. Clambering over him, she slid off his side of the bed and crouched on the floor to attack the ropes.

"You bent your wrists?"

"Yes," she replied distractedly, struggling with his bonds. "Then I unbent them and slipped my hands through the ropes. Oh, Josh, these knots are so tight! And you're bleeding!"

"I'll live. Where did you learn that little trick?"

"What trick? Oh, the bent wrists. From the diary of Captain Sir Giles Pettibone. He was captured by Barbary Coast pirates. They tied him up every night, but he eventually escaped and . . . I think this knot is loosening!"

Josh was grinning by the time she'd worked the ropes enough for him to slide his hands through. Leave it to Cari to find a solution in her history books. Jackknifing off the bed, he knelt beside her on the floor and cupped her face in his hands.

"Remind me to read old Pettibone's diary when we get home. I want to know what other tricks you learned."

"What makes you think you're going to have time to read anything when we get home?"

The flash of mischief in her brown eyes made Josh ache to kiss her. Instead, he drew in a deep breath. This wasn't the time or the place for declarations, but he wasn't taking any chances. They weren't home free. Not by a long shot. But no matter what happened, he had to tell her the thoughts that had whirled through his mind these past hours.

"I meant what I said a while ago," he said urgently. "I love you. More than I ever thought it possible to love another human being."

"Me too."

"I don't want a divorce."

She shook her head, smiling. "Me neither."

"I don't have much to offer you right now. I don't even know if I'll have any income coming in for a while."

"I don't care. I can earn enough to keep us in pizza and plant food. That's all we'll need until you get your swing back."

Josh blinked. Obviously the term "not much to offer" was a relative one. To him, it meant he wouldn't be able to provide Cari with the kind of freewheeling big-money life-style that came from standing in the winner's circle. To her, it boiled down to the basics in life.

But they both knew there was more at stake here than pizza and plant food.

"I might not ever get my swing back," he told her evenly. "Hell, I couldn't even see well enough to hit Paxton a while ago, and he was standing just a few feet away."

Her hands came up to cover his. "Josh, listen to me. I understand that you're at a critical point in your professional life, that you may not be able to play golf again the way you did before. I wish I could help you through that, but I can't. All I can do is tell you that I love you. Whatever comes, we'll face it together."

"It's not just my life we're talking about here. You're at a critical point in your career, too."

She tilted her head as a host of emotions chased across her expressive face. Josh saw acknowledgment, resignation, and fierce determination.

"I still want to complete my degree," she said, her eyes on his face. "If it takes me five or seven or ten years longer than I'd planned, then it takes me another five or seven or ten years. I can accept that, if it means I'll spend those years with you."

Josh couldn't help himself. She looked so serious, so fierce.

"Just think of all the costumes you can come up with during those years, sweetheart," he teased. "As much as I enjoyed playing pirate and bride and groom with you, I have this sudden urge to see you as a harem slave, with an emerald in your belly button and rings on every one of your sexy little toes..."

"Josh, for heaven sakes!"

"...and not much in between," he finished, grinning broadly.

"We'd better make sure we have five or seven or ten years left to play any games at all," she retorted.

"We will," he promised, as determined now as she'd been a moment ago. Then he kissed her. Gingerly, given his split lip, but very, very hungrily. She clung to him, her arms tight around his neck, as though she wouldn't ever let him go.

Reluctantly Josh reached up to loosen her arms. When he saw the smears on her cheeks left by his bloodied hands, reality came crashing back with a vengeance. His jaw tightening, he helped her up.

"We need to plan our attack."

"Attack?" she squeaked. "Shouldn't we just wait till Enrique comes back and, er, ambush him? You know, two against one?"

He shook his head. "There's no guarantee he'll come back alone. We can't take that chance. We have to get out and warn the other passengers. There are ten of us, and, what—four crew members?"

She nodded. "The captain, Enrique, the chef, and the woman who cleans the cabins. The chef's wife." Her eyes wide, Cari stared at him. "Oh, Josh, do you think they're in on this smuggling, too?"

"We have to assume they are. Look around the cabin. See what you can find to use as a weapon."

As she searched, Cari's bravado of moments before faded. Suddenly the huge cabin seemed much more a haven than the prison she'd considered it for the past few hours. She wasn't cut out for adventure on the high seas, she admitted to herself. Given the choice between going topside to take out some twentieth-century brigands and cowering in her own bed with the covers over her head, she knew exactly which she'd choose. Assuming she could have Josh under the covers with her.

He, on the other hand, searched the cabin with a grim determination that bordered on eagerness. When he hefted a heavy red-sealed bottle of Scotch and smacked it against his palm, his lips drew back in a feral smile.

"I can't think of a better use for the captain's red-label bar stock than to crack it over his head," he murmured. "Let's hope I can get close enough to—"

He broke off, his entire body tensing as he cocked his head, listening intently.

"Oh, God!" Cari whispered. "Enrique's coming back already?"

She turned and raced across the room. With a leap, she threw herself on the bed. Maybe she could act as a decoy for a few precious seconds. Just long enough to lure the steward far enough into the room for Josh to get a clear swing at him. She jerked her arms behind her and stared at the door, wide-eyed and trembling.

To her considerable surprise, Josh ignored the main entrance to the suite and crossed to the sliding glass doors. He halted a few feet away, back flattened against the wall beside the curtains that covered the doors. The tic that had fascinated Cari so much just last night beat a furious tattoo in the side of his jaw.

Her blood was hammering so loudly in her ears that she almost missed the faint scratching at the glass. Swallowing, she stared at the curtains. Josh's brows slashed down at the sound. He hefted the bottle of Scotch higher.

The scratching came again, and then a faint whisper.

"Josh?"

Cari and Josh looked at each other, suspicion and hope warring on their faces. She held her breath as he reached out and lifted the edge of the curtain an infinitesimal fraction. When Josh flashed her a grin and lowered his weapon, her pent-up breath came out in a sob. A moment later, he unlatched the sliding glass doors and Eric slipped inside.

The boy took one look at Josh's face and whistled softly. "I told Granddad there was something funny going on this morning!"

"How did you know?"

The teenager snorted. "Enrique's face had something to do with it."

"Smart kid."

"Yeah, well, I didn't think much about it until you didn't show up for our golf lesson this morning. The captain made some joke about you and Cari being on your honeymoon, but, jeez! You've been on your honeymoon for a week now, and . . . Well, this is *golf* we're talking about."

"So it is," Josh replied, grinning at Cari over the boy's head.

She shimmied off the bed and came over to join the other two. "How did you get down to our deck?"

"I climbed down the awning support," Eric replied with a shrug, as if the answer should be obvious to anyone, even a history teacher. "Granddad's keeping watch up on the sun deck right now."

Josh gripped the boy's shoulder. "Eric, are the clubs still there? Up on the sun deck?"

"Yeah. Why?"

He chewed on his lower lip for a moment, then tugged the boy around to face him. "I want you to stay here with Cari while your granddad and I go see the captain. I need you to protect her," he added, stifling the boy's protest. "So I don't have to worry about her during my . . . discussion with the captain."

The look he sent Cari stifled her protest, as well. Her job was to keep Eric out of danger. She understood it. She accepted it. But she didn't like it. At all. Consequently, she was as nervous and tight-lipped as Eric when Josh slid the glass door open and stepped out onto the small private deck.

Josh stood in the shadow of the awning, his pulse pounding. Astern, the *Nautilus III* churned a wake of white lace against a sparkling sea. Overhead, gulls whirled in an endless azure sky. He shuffled sideways an inch, then another. Craning his neck, he peered over the edge of the awning.

To his intense relief, he spied Paul Sanders's beefy, balding figure leaning against the rail of the sun deck.

It was over so quickly, Josh felt cheated. He wanted blood. He wanted the satisfaction of smashing his fists into Enrique's face. He wanted Paxton on his knees.

He got one good swing in. Enrique howled like a gored bull when Josh slammed an iron down on his wrist and sent the gun skittering across the deck. Paul Sanders scooped up the gun and trained it on the man with a skill that told Josh the cement business bred some tough customers.

The two men then put the steward out cold without the least compunction. Leaving him securely tied and under the supervision of another club-wielding passenger, he led a small army of vigilante executives to the bridge.

Faced with the business end of Enrique's gun, Paxton surrendered without a fight. A quick search showed that the chef and his wife were unarmed and totally astounded by the turn of events. Still, to be safe, Josh kept the couple under guard alongside Paxton and Enrique. Then he faced the group of well-dressed men and women who were left to operate the ship.

"Anyone here know how to drive a yacht?"

"I've got a boat at home," one of the passengers volunteered. "It's just a thirty-footer, but what the hell? That's only a hundred and twenty feet or so shorter than this baby."

Josh sketched him a salute. "She's all yours, Captain. At least until the Coast Guard arrives."

Six hours later, the *Nautilus III* glided gracefully toward a long wooden pier stretching out into Georgetown's harbor.

Clutching at the rail, Cari stared in dismay at the crowd jammed onto the pier. The entire population of Grand Cayman Island must have congregated to greet them, as well as every international reporter in the Caribbean.

As the engines reversed and the *Nautilus* shuddered to a slow halt at quayside, camera crews jostled with sound handlers for position. Reporters with bags slung over their shoulders elbowed each other aside. Shouts rang across the fast shrinking distance.

"Josh! Hey, Josh!"

"Over here, Keegan!"

The man at Cari's side lifted a hand and gave them a friendly wave. She could only marvel at his sangfroid.

He'd warned her that their distress signal had been picked up by ships of several different nationalities. That the story had no doubt gone flashing over the network satellites before the high-speed Coast Guard cutter cruising off Haiti came to their aid. She'd expected media interest, but not this . . . this frenzy.

She shivered at the thought of facing this horde. An instant later, an arm slipped around her waist.

"Kind of intimidating, isn't it?"

"There's no 'kind of' about it."

Josh cocked his head, smiling down at her. "Remember what I told you about handling the media? You tell them what you want them to hear, and listen selectively to what they say or print about you."

"I've got a better idea. You tell them what you want them to hear. I'll sneak ashore later."

Laughter rumbled up from deep in his chest. "No way, sweetheart. We're in this thing together, remember?"

His words went a long way toward shoring up Cari's frayed nerves. Unfortunately, he accompanied them with a long, slow, knee-bending kiss that delighted their audience and totally destroyed Cari's tenuous composure. She clung to him with both hands, barely able to breathe, while a chorus of catcalls and whistles rose from the pier.

When the yacht bumped gently against its padded berth a few moments later, she was still trying to draw air into her starved lungs. Josh glanced down at her, his signature grin lifting one corner of his mouth.

"Ready?"

"No." She sighed. "But I suppose we'll have to face them before we can go ashore and try to find an emerald to fit my belly button."

The look in his hazel eye made Cari's toes curl. Her sexy little toes, according to Josh.

"This is going to be one of the shortest news conferences in history."

She was basking in the heat of his promise when the passengers began to congregate at the gangplank that bridged the short space to the pier.

"Cari!"

Evelyn Sanders edged her way through the perfumed crowd. Diamonds glistened at her ears, and another huge stone weighted her ring finger. From the eager anticipation on her face, it was obvious the older woman was looking forward to her moment in front of the cameras.

"With all the excitement, I almost forgot to give you this!" Beaming, she passed Cari a ribboned box. "It's not much. Just a little memento from Paul and Eric and me. I hope you like it."

Cari fumbled with the ribbon, then lifted the lid. When she saw the photograph framed in crystal and silver, she gave a gasp of sheer delight.

"Oh, Evelyn! Thank you!"

Her eyes misting, Cari studied the shot of her and Josh cutting their wedding cake. Her groom stood behind her, tall and solid and incredibly handsome in his ivory linen jacket and light blue shirt. The sea breeze ruffled his dark hair, and his mouth curved in a teasing grin that was all Josh.

Cari's heart overflowed, and she was sure she couldn't love him any more than she did right now.

She was wrong.

Moments later, she stood beside him on the pier. He fielded the melee of shouts and questions with a good-natured ease that amazed Cari.

"What's this about you taking out a whole band of smugglers with a one iron, Josh?"

His warm, rich laughter flowed across the pier. "As Lee Trevino says, only God can hit a one iron. I used a two."

"We saw that kiss a few moments ago, Keegan," someone at the back of the crowd called. "Who's the mystery lady?"

Josh glanced down at Cari, his faced filled with a tenderness that made her clutch Evelyn's gift to her breast.

"The lady is my wife."

Epilogue

The front door of Gulliver's Travels flew open. Tiffany Tarrington Toulouse dashed in, her cheeks bright and her wild mane of silvery-white curls tossed by the chill November wind.

"Lucy! Jimmy! Everyone! Did you see the paper this morning?"

Her breathless excitement brought Lucy Falco from the coffee maker, and Jim Burns from his computer. The other travel agents put phones on hold and gathered in the center of the spacious work center, peering over Tiffany's shoulder as she whipped open a folded newspaper.

"Look, it's Josh Keegan and the woman he met at the Halloween charity ball. You remember the mock ceremony you told us about, Lucy? The one they participated in?"

"How could I forget?" Lucy replied, smiling. "Every woman at the ball, me included, sighed in sheer, unadulterated envy when Josh said, 'I do,' even though it was all a gag."

"It wasn't a gag! They're really married! And they took advantage of the cruise package Jimmy put together to go on their honeymoon."

"No kidding?" The former short-order cook turned used-car salesman turned travel agent gaped at the UPI photo of Atlanta's best-known bachelor with an arm around the woman identified as his bride.

"But what's all this about modern-day pirates and drama on the high seas?" Lucy asked, her dark brows slanting as she tilted her head to read the upside-down headlines.

Tiffany's eyes danced with a liveliness that belied her sixty-plus years. "Well, it seems the honey of a deal Jimmy worked out on this cruise wasn't quite as sweet as we thought. The captain gave us such a tremendous discount because he was using the cruise business as a front for a drug smuggling operation."

"Drug smuggling!" Lucy's eyes widened in dismay. "We sent Josh Keegan and...and his wife off on a ten-day cruise aboard a boat involved in drug running?"

Jimmy groaned. "Oh, no. When Mr. Gulliver hears about this, I'm going to be back hustling used cars!"

Snatching the paper from Tiffany's ringed hands, Lucy absorbed the details of the situation they'd unknowingly thrust two clients into. At least no one was hurt, she read with a surge of relief. She glanced at the photo again, her tension easing as caught the glowing look on the bride's face. Remembering Cari O'Donnell's stormy expression when she'd accepted the prize package in the hotel lobby Halloween night, Lucy came to the conclusion that more had happened on that cruise than either the bride or groom had shared with the press.

"I'll talk to Mr. Gulliver," she assured the anxious Jim Burns. "The boss will understand that you couldn't possibly know about the drug running."

Lucy had worked for the elusive entrepreneur for several years now, communicating with him primarily via phone and fax. He wouldn't be happy about this, but he wasn't arbitrary or unfair.

Her smile encompassed the rest of the small group. "We all need to take a lesson from this experience. Let's make sure we don't put together any more honeymoon packages quite this . . . exciting. Stick to our tried-and-true carriers and resorts."

"I'm working on another package right now," a wide-eyed Tiffany put in. "I've got a soldier flying home from overseas on leave. A small Thanksgiving wedding. A honeymoon at an old established lodge. Nice, safe and traditional. We can't go wrong with this one."

"I hope not," Lucy replied, her glance lingering on the photograph of Cari and Josh Keegan. "I sincerely hope not."

*   *   *   *   *

The spirit of the holidays...
The magic of romance...
They both come together in

You're invited as Merline Lovelace and Carole Buck—
two of your favorite authors from two of your favorite
lines—capture your hearts with five joyous love stories
celebrating the excitement that happens when you
combine holidays and weddings!

Beginning in October, watch for

HALLOWEEN HONEYMOON by Merline Lovelace
(Desire #1030, 10/96)

Thanksgiving—
WRONG BRIDE, RIGHT GROOM by Merline Lovelace
(Desire #1037, 11/96)

Christmas—
A BRIDE FOR SAINT NICK by Carole Buck
(Intimate Moments #752, 12/96)

New Year's Day—
RESOLVED TO (RE)MARRY by Carole Buck
(Desire #1049, 1/97)

Valentine's Day—
THE 14TH...AND FOREVER by Merline Lovelace
(Intimate Moments #764, 2/97)

Silhouette®
™

1997
Reader's Engagement Book
A calendar of important dates
and anniversaries for readers to use!

Informative and entertaining—with notable
dates and trivia highlighted throughout the year.

Handy, convenient, pocketbook size to help you
keep track of your own personal important dates.

Added bonus—contains $5.00 worth of coupons
for upcoming Harlequin and Silhouette books.
This calendar more than pays for itself!

Available beginning in November at
your favorite retail outlet.

For the Janos siblings

Three Weddings and a Gift

leads to a lot of loving!
Join award-winning author

Cathie Linz

as she shows how an *unusual* inheritance leads to
love at first sight—and beyond!—in

MICHAEL'S BABY #1023
September 1996

SEDUCING HUNTER #1029
October 1996

and

ABBIE AND THE COWBOY #1036
November 1996

Only from

SILHOUETTE®

Desire

This October, be the first to read these wonderful
authors as they make their dazzling debuts!

Women to Watch

THE WEDDING KISS by Robin Wells
(Silhouette Romance #1185)
A reluctant bachelor rescues the woman he loves
from the man she's about to marry—and turns into
a willing groom himself!

THE SEX TEST by Patty Salier
(Silhouette Desire #1032)
A pretty professor learns there's more to making love
than meets the eye when she takes lessons from
a sexy stranger.

IN A FAMILY WAY by Julia Mozingo
(Special Edition #1062)
A woman without a past finds shelter in the arms of
a handsome rancher. Can she trust him to protect
her unborn child?

UNDER COVER OF THE NIGHT by Roberta Tobeck
(Intimate Moments #744)
A rugged government agent encounters the woman he has
always loved. But past secrets could threaten their future.

DATELESS IN DALLAS by Samantha Carter
(Yours Truly)
A hapless reporter investigates how to find the perfect
mate—and winds up falling for her handsome rival!

Don't miss the brightest stars of tomorrow!

Only from **Silhouette®**